Kim and Jim

The Length of Love Street

Jim Blyth

Boorach Books

Published by Boorach Books, 2014
www.boorachbooks.com

ISBN: 978-0-9926033-3-5

Cover illustration by Tanja Russita. See more of
Tanja's work at www.tanjarussita.com

If you like this book, please help us to spread the
word about it by leaving a review at the book's
Amazon page!

We are always happy to hear your feedback on
info@boorachbooks.com

Kim & Jim

The Length of Love Street

Easter Holiday Weekend

Paisley

2001

Chapter 1

It's Easter Friday and it's raining

1.1

It's Easter Friday and it's raining.
They think, when will it ever end?
No point in sitting here complaining,
Driving each other round the bend.
We should have gone to Barcelona,
To see our old friends, Pete and Shona.
How often have they phoned and said
'Jump on a plane. You'll have a bed?'
Not that their home is such displeasure,
Just empty now the kids have flown
The nest. How suddenly they'd grown.
And now, with too much time for leisure,
And too young to be laid to rest,
They don't know what to do for best.

1.2

It caused no little consternation,
On reaching this point in their life,
To realise their appellation
Was father, mother; husband, wife;
Defined not by themselves, but others:
Their son and daughter; sisters, brothers;
Defined not by themselves, but those
They gave birth to, and fed and clothed.
'What were the names with which we're christened?
If I remember, mine was Jim.
My lifetime partner's? Hers was Kim.'
However hard you might have listened,
They'd not been heard round here of late;
The names of Jim and his best mate.

1.3
They sit in silence at the table
And watch terrestrial TV.
They're too old fashioned to have cable,
And get their news from BBC.
Tomorrow's World and then Eastenders;
A Cook Report on moneylenders.
She pours another glass of fizz,
Filling her own, ignoring his.
He stands to clear away the curry.
There's not much left. A ready meal
For working couples is ideal.
She turns and says 'Shh! Will you hurry!'
Then turns the volume up to nine
To catch the start of Gardening Time.

1.4
Jim scans the TV pages, mapping
The evening's viewing after ten,
Then sits with fingers idly tapping ...
Remote control is hers till then.
They'll sit for one and a half hours
Through talk of plants and weeds and flowers,
And when they've finished talk of blooms,
They'll watch two couples changing rooms.
As entertainment goes, it's painful,
He thinks with melancholy sigh;
It's truly watching wet paint dry.
But watch he does, with look disdainful,
The happy chap who fronts the show
Tell how to make our gardens grow.

1.5
He steps out from behind some rigging,
Lays down the plans he'd like to see.
Two cheery teuchters do the digging
And shift the earth from A to B.
They hear their horticultural teachers
Extol the joys of water features;
Of plants from far exotic climes;
Of pergolas, bamboo and chimes.
Outside, a couple pass by, necking:
Long-standing adolescent right
Of passage on a Friday night.
Inside, they're stuck with wooden decking
And how to make the garden shed
Blend in with a raised flower bed.

1.6
Jim thinks of when they, too, were winching;
When love was innocent and tame;
His hand beneath her jumper, inching
Slowly across her slender frame.
His aim? Her bra, and how to breach it.
It took him seven weeks to reach it.
And when he crossed the finishing line,
She said 'Well, well, you took your time!'
He found this strange and quite surprising:
The last girl, when he'd reached her strap,
Administered a hefty slap.
For weeks he was apologising.
The poor lad didn't really know
Whether a boy should come, or go!

1.7

Oh, where on earth have Fridays vanished?
I don't think we were always old.
Our spicy, hot Madras is banished,
Replaced by korma that's gone cold.
Though korma has a homely flavour
It's not the menu that I favour;
A wishy-washy kind of taste
That needs a dose of curry paste;
An extra chilli, coriander,
Some cloves or ginger in the mix
Would go some way to adding kicks.
Without, the recipe is blander,
No tang or tingle on the lips.
We'd be as well with oven chips.

1.8

Too much time spent beside the telly
Affects us all in certain ways:
A gradual swelling of the belly
Takes place over reclining days.
In tandem, as the waist increases,
Our brain cells start to fall to pieces;
Bombarded by the cathode rays,
Both eyes, in time, are double-glazed.
Communication's one-way traffic,
All information coming in;
Our minds become a rubbish bin.
Our social skills' decline is graphic;
Harder and harder to connect,
Communication lines are wrecked.

1.9

Her he-mail fails to get reaction;
His she-mail genders no reply.
Their server must be out of action
With no help desk to tell them why.
And, having left the problem lying,
It seems the two have just stopped trying.
The lack of useful IT skills
Has left them stranded with their ills.
The system's not completely broken:
An engineer would soon repair
The workings that are all still there,
But any effort's purely token.
There simply doesn't seem to be
The will to press the enter key.

1.10

Meanwhile, the gardening utensils
Are tidied up and put away;
Pale pastel paints and patterned stencils
Are thrown in to the cassoulet.
The show's presenter pouts and gushes;
A decorator primes his brushes;
Designers with artistic flair
Theatrically flick their hair,
Expound their views on current fashion,
On what is in, and what is not,
On what is cool, and what is hot,
Indulging in a fervent passion
For textures, fabrics, tiles and rugs,
Assorted junk and Toby jugs.

1.11
Two unsuspecting couples hover,
Each offering up their own abode:
A turf accountant and his lover;
Two teachers from across the road.
They set to work with gay abandon,
Forgetting all the things they'd planned on,
And understated shades of blue
Take on distinctly purple hue.
The joiner's given his instructions,
But, whistling, makes pretend he's deaf
And hammers on some MDF,
Wondering how these odd constructions,
Made out of tin foil, scrap and wood,
Can be considered any good.

1.12
It's all in all a strange confection,
At least to Jim's uncultured eye.
Inherent faults escape detection,
So obvious, he can't think why
The householders appear delighted
At having had their front rooms blighted.
The artisans wipe sweated brow.
Flapping designers take a bow.
Kim marvels at the use of colour.
'That's what we need to do in here.
You must admit, it's pretty drear,
It couldn't really be much duller.
A touch of pink, some navy blue
Would be quite nice, I think. Don't you?

1.13
'This room is really such a hovel.
It's been like this the last ten years.
Better to take a pick and shovel,
Knock the whole lot around our ears,
Rebuild in fashion more in keeping
With modern tastes. Jim, are you sleeping?
Have you heard one word I've said?
God, it's like talking to the dead.'
She bends down, taking off her trainer,
Throwing it at her husband's head,
But hits the goldfish bowl instead,
Causing the spherical container
To fall directly in his lap,
Bringing him sharply from his nap

1.14
To witness a small pool of water
Forming below him, on the mat;
And see the goldfish of his daughter
Be swallowed by the family cat.
Licking her lips in satisfaction,
She sits and gauges their reaction.
Jim thinks it must all be a dream,
Till Kim lets out an angry scream:
'It's your fault that we've lost our guppy.
Poor Kate has had the thing for years.
When she finds out, she'll be in tears.
We'll need to go and buy a puppy.'
Jim goes to say, 'To hell with that,
Better to shoot the bloody cat'

1.15

But holds his tongue. He senses trouble
Is winging his way from afar.
He doesn't need to look through Hubble
To see what's written in his stars.
A prehistoric instinct grips him,
Its voice, through primal channels, tips him
To hold quite still and make no sound,
As mortal danger lies around.
And so, ruled by primeval psyche,
He sits there, frozen, in his chair,
Feeling the coolness in the air,
And wonders how his partner's Nike
Came to be sitting on the shelf,
A few inches above himself.

1.16

What could have caused the chain reaction
That made the shoe fly through the air?
He's pretty sure his own inaction
Could not have made it settle there.
How did his jeans receive a soaking?
Why was the goldfish beached and croaking?
Who made him look like a drowned rat?
Was all this caused by a mere cat?
When Kim takes off her other trainer,
The cat gives out a squeal of fright
And dashes out the line of flight,
In case her mistress tries to brain her;
But seeing the shoe flung on the floor,
Moves haughtily towards the door

1.17

And, quietly, with presidential
Aloofness, slips out the house,
Leaving Jim there to face potential
Hostile reaction from his spouse.
In keeping out of the hiatus,
She has retained her neutral status,
So when her owners' fighting ends,
They both can still be feline friends.
For she has learned that she who judges,
In offering support to one,
Will find, when arguments are done,
The other's likely to bear grudges.
And it is no fun being a mog
When people treat you like a dog.

1.18

Jim cannot hold his peace much longer.
Several minutes now have passed,
And his desire to speak grows stronger
By the minute, until, at last,
He decides that negotiation
Should help resolve the situation.
A deftly chosen word or phrase
Can solve the toughest moral maze.
He'd once been on a course at college,
Learning how to appease life's ills
Through good communication skills.
And drawing on his boundless knowledge,
He gives the matter careful thought,
Then blurts defensively, 'Well? What?'

1.19
'Well? What? Is that your contribution
Towards the evening's whole debate?
It's not much of a resolution
To that poor wee goldfish's fate.
But, then again, it's quite in keeping
With all your usual lack of speaking.
Sometimes, Jim, when we sit at home,
You make me feel I'm so alone.'
She pauses, as if quite affected,
Suddenly, by the things she's said.
Such thoughts had long been in her head,
Though by the world, quite undetected.
Now, what had languished safe, concealed,
Unto her partner was revealed.

1.20
And in that simple thought's expression,
She discovers that what had been,
In her own mind, a mild depression:
Just boredom really, with routine,
Of working, sleeping, washing dishes,
—There'd be no further feeding fishes—
The days when you could write the text,
When one would merge into the next,
Perhaps was more a plainer issue,
Nothing to do with ailing health
Or any ghosts inside herself.
And, reaching down, she lifts a tissue,
Gently wiping away a tear,
And draws her hair behind her ear.

1.21

'It's hard to have a conversation
With you. You seem so far away.
And I can get no indication
That you can hear a word I say.
Do you care how my day is going?
Can it be such a hardship knowing?
Is this the reason marriage ends:
That if you're mates, you can't be friends?'
Thus Jim's discomfiture increases:
Both at the tone of Kim's retorts,
And soaked through to his boxer shorts.
So, when her heartfelt pleading ceases,
He thinks how he can best reply.
He doesn't like to see her cry.

1.22

'Well, just because I killed the goldfish
—And I am not convinced of that —
It doesn't make me such a cold fish.'
—I bet it was the bloody cat—
'It's more than that, Jim, and you know it.
You've got a brain: why don't you show it,
Rather than juvenile pretence,
Just making jokes and acting dense?
And just because a person threatens
To uncover your inner thoughts,
Your tongue just ties itself in knots.
Oh, sometimes men are total cretins!
You are the one with a degree.
So, how come you can't talk to me?'

1.23

The threat of tears has now receded.
Well, for the moment, anyway.
And Kim decides that what is needed
Is a large glass of Cabernet;
Perhaps a light Valpollicella;
A Shiraz from a New-World cellar;
The usual pick-me-up required,
Whenever she feels sad, or tired.
She finds one meeting her approval
In the stair cupboard in the hall.
She lifts the opener from the wall
And engineers the cork's removal
With all the speed of one who's skilled,
And pours until her glass is filled

1.24

Up to the brim; sets down the bottle
By her feet; then she carries on.
'You don't need to be Aristotle
To figure out that something's wrong,
Or have the cerebrum of Plato
To stop being a couch potato.
And no Homeric Odyssey
Is needed to come back to me.'
And then, with glass raised, she says 'Yamas!'
With an ironic, muffled laugh.
'I'm going upstairs for a bath;
And then I'll put on my pyjamas,
My slippers and my dressing gown.
And be assured … I'll be back down.'

1.25

So she departs with the remainder
Of the bottle, and slams the door.
'Mmm. Something I've done must have pained her
And hurt her to her very core.
But I can't figure out too clearly
What I have done. Here am I, merely
At rest from five long days of toil,
And I'm just making her blood boil.
But now, my jeans and shorts need changing;
It looks as though I've wet myself.
I'll put the bowl back on the shelf.
The cushions will need rearranging.
I'll put these damp bits to the rear,
And then I'll get myself a beer.'

1.26

He ambles over to the window
To draw the curtains for the night,
Stopping to listen to the wind blow.
Looks like the forecast could be right,
For strong north winds and scattered showers.
Oh, what a joy, this land of ours.
Easter weekend and, true to form,
We're all still waiting for the warm.
Yet, though the good days can be fleeting,
Thermostatically controlled,
The Scottish weather can be tholed.
He bends down and adjusts the heating
Upwards by one degree or two,
Then clears up the offending shoe.

1.27

He unbuttons his Levi Strausses,
And slips them off; they're damp right through.
With curtains drawn, he's safe as houses,
Protected from his neighbours' view.
He lays them on the radiator
To dry; he'll put them back on later.
Then goes to get himself a beer,
To pass the time till she appears.
He sets off in his socks and jumper
Towards the kitchen, where his cache
Of finest ales is proudly stashed;
Although his stocks are hardly bumper,
As beer retention can be tough
When you so like to drink the stuff.

1.28

With pint of lager, or of Heavy,
The choice most drinkers used to face,
Jim's cupboard housed exotic bevvy.
Each week, his friends would meet to taste
Dark Irish stout and English bitter,
Best Belhaven and strong Skullsplitter,
And finish with Old Speckled Hen.
Then, next week, they'd begin again.
Alas, these days he's faring badly,
For there's a smaller choice on view.
In fact, it's just a choice of two.
He looks at his collection sadly
And settles on the Special Brew;
Then picks the other one up too.

1.29
Back through the house, the TV's blaring
On regardless; he sits back down.
Conscious of what he isn't wearing,
He pulls a pair of cushions round
The little bits that now are feeling
Rather exposed and unappealing,
Needing a place where they can hide.
He places one on either side;
He then picks up the bean bag, lying
Down by the fire, and places it
On his most vulnerable bit.
Soft furnishings thus dignifying
His unclad state, he lifts a tin,
Opens his mouth and pours some in.

1.30
On screen, the football's just beginning;
Firstly reviewing last week's card,
Who all had lost and who was winning,
Who all had scored and who had starred.
And, now that Easter was upon us,
The big teams battled for the honours,
While all the others would confess
That mere survival meant success.
Jim followed St Mirren. Quite plainly
Not the choice of a reasoned mind,
As good times there were hard to find.
And yet, he'd kept the faith, insanely
Letting his frail emotions be
Wrung out each Saturday at three.

1.31

All through the world, the Tannahill Weavers'
Paisley Patterns had made their mark.
The new coach had the fans believers,
That they'd see artwork on the park.
But all the promise was a phantom.
In fact, the patterns seemed quite random,
Their new defender's hefty dunt
Weaving a pattern back to front;
And rather than a style artistic,
Focused on skill and measured pass,
Skimming smartly across the grass,
The tactics were to go ballistic,
Hoping a team-mate would be there
When ball descended from the air.

1.32

And, sure to say, the unsuccessful
Tactics led to the coach being fired.
But Saturdays were no less stressful
When a new manager was hired.
And so the wheel, full-circle spinning,
Left the team as before … not winning.
A long time hence, he'd ceased to go
To any games. The radio
Kept scorelines to his satisfaction.
But, though an age since he had been,
When younger, he had been so keen
To be a part of all the action.
And he had travelled to and fro:
To Shawfield, Firhill, Cappielow.

1.33

All names to conjure up rare visions:
To Somerset, Fir, Ochilview.
He travelled through the old divisions,
Up and back down from one to two.
But youthful keenness grew half-hearted
And over time, had then departed.
He followed on his team no more,
Beyond the age of twenty-four.
He's still a fan, after a fashion.
Even although he's never there,
He gives support from his armchair;
But Love Street has not felt his passion,
Or seen his face inside the gate,
Since nineteen …what …seventy-eight?

1.34

He sits and wonders what became of
The mates with whom he used to go:
Peter and Bill, and what's the name of
That guy who sometimes came with Joe?
He can't remember. Doesn't matter.
The fun was mainly just the patter.
All meeting in the pub at one,
And, late out, having then to run
The length of Love Street, laughing, puffing,
Reaching the ground, no time to spare,
Through the turnstiles and up the stair
To watch our favourites get a cuffing,
—As was too many times the case—
And, ten to five, head back to base.

1.35
Musing on all those old adventures
Makes him consider going again,
Although he's heard it's now debentures;
Corporate boxes; business men,
With knowledge of financial sectors,
Who're wined and dined by club directors,
Attracting new-found income streams
To save underperforming teams.
 Up on the screen, he spots the fixture
List. Who is it St Mirren play?
Heart of Midlothian: away.
And soon, with unfamiliar mixture
Of quick decision-making and
Nostalgia, finds his day is planned.

1.36
'I'll be at work at half-past seven;
The year-end stock-take to complete.
We should be finished by eleven;
Meet Kim and grab a bite to eat.
Then Gilmour Street to Glasgow Central,
On up to Queen Street, then a gentle
Run through to Haymarket by train.
No point by car, parking's a pain.
I'll watch the match. Kim can go shopping.
At five o'clock, meet up again.
Some food, some drinks, back home by ten.
First, though, I should consider dropping
Some hints to how I plan the day;
To get her onside, as they say.'

Chapter 2

There's just one minor flaw, however

2.1

There's just one minor flaw, however,
Contained within this plan of his.
And though he thinks it fairly clever,
Things are about to go amiss.
While he is lounging downstairs, drinking,
His spouse is lying upstairs, thinking.
She's also hatched a little plot
And, one thing that's for sure, it's not
In any way concerned with going
Out to a football match with Jim,
For she has other plans for him:
Some digging, weeding, planting, hoeing,
And turning that back garden round.
It's such an ugly piece of ground.

2.2

All overgrown and unattended,
A patchy, moss-filled piece of grass.
Some slatted fence that's needing mended,
Some scattered stones and broken glass.
That is, at least, depending whether
On Saturday there's drier weather
Than Friday's seen; for, if there's rain,
Then gardening would be in vain.
If so, then plan B would be active:
To tackle the pervading gloom
Of their old lived-in living room,
Which once was not so unattractive,
But now, while hardly trashed or wrecked,
Is suffering from distinct neglect.

2.3

Her weekend's plan thus formulated,
Now Kim is quite surprised to find
Her temper, in the main, abated,
Soothed fully by both bath and wine.
In thinking of her unkempt garden,
A new resolve begins to harden.
For too long she has stood aside
And watched the inexorable slide.
Is it too late to be untangled?
She realises, in dismay,
That the slow process of decay,
Unchecked, has all the flora strangled,
Choking it of its very breath
And now has left it close to death.

2.4

Kim suddenly begins to shiver.
She stands up and pulls out the plug.
Her arms and shoulders briefly quiver
As she steps out on to the rug.
Thinking of all that garden rubble,
Immersed within her soapy bubble,
Must have passed half an hour, all told,
And now the water has gone cold.
So deep in her deliberation
She'd been, she'd hardly noticed that
The bubbles were completely flat.
And, adding to her irritation,
Dripping wet and completely bare,
She finds there's not a towel there.

2.5

She quickly pads across the landing
Into the bedroom, shuts the door
And sees the pile of ironing standing
Beside the wardrobe, on the floor,
Just where she'd dumped it, Tuesday teatime,
And since when she had had no free time.
Well, she'd had some, but what the hell …
She needs time to relax as well.
Ironing is her biggest loathing,
Frequently lying up the stair
Till someone needs a shirt to wear.
Among the pile of crumpled clothing
She quickly rakes, pulls out a red
Hand towel, for around her head,

2.6

But then she stops. Her own reflection
In the mirror has caught her gaze,
And she begins a quick inspection
Of all her bodywork, and face.
'I think I've still a youthful figure,
Although in places it is bigger;
Mirror, mirror, tell me no lies.
Just what has happened to my thighs?
I seem to have some thermal lagging.
And I just thought my jeans had shrunk.
It must be all that wine I've drunk.
At least my boobs are far from sagging;
They're still as firm at forty-three
As on the day he married me.'

2.7
And as she clasps her bosom gently,
Her gaze moves down, across her girth,
Down to her stomach, evidently
The source of pained Caesarean birth.
And tracing downward with her fingers
Where still the soft scar tissue lingers,
And down across, around her hips,
Silently, with her fingertips,
She maps her every year of living:
Every hollow and every rise,
A witness to each day that dies;
Each lovely sunset, unforgiving,
Painted across the evening sky,
Another day that's passed her by.

2.8
Oh, how we take our youth for granted
When we are young. We just don't know.
And then, by middle age supplanted
Overnight — at least it seems so.
What have we then to look ahead to?
Can this be all our lives have led to:
Stripped of all our ambition's dress,
Solitude in our nakedness?
And what of all the dreams we dreamed then?
Some had come true, but most expired;
The bulk were alcohol-inspired!
But unto all around, it seemed, then,
That there was never limit to
What we could think of, or could do.

2.9

And now? What is it motivates us?
Trying to be like we were then?
How this obsesses, captivates us:
To look as we once did, again.
We're chasing non-existent prizes
In quite ridiculous disguises,
And end, predictably, this race
With sheepish smile on foolish face.
But, if she did, then who could blame her
For trying to counter time's advance?
Should she sit, passively entranced?
Yet, still her body does not shame her.
In full flush of her womanhood,
She knows its way, and feels it good

2.10

To know what it will take to please her.
She's confident in who she is.
Yet once, uncertainty would seize her:
Did her backside look big in this?
Should she diet? Perhaps be thinner?
Would people see a saint or sinner?
Was she too ugly? Was she fat?
And should her hair be high or flat?
And so, in confidence diminished,
She would decry her very self:
'I'm sure to be left on the shelf!'
Just seventeen, and life was finished!
The tortures that we all endure
That only passing years can cure!

2.11

'So, being young … not all plain sailing,'
She mutters with a rueful smile.
With luck, her body won't be failing
Her, hopefully, for quite a while.
What it needs right now, though, is cover,
And from a cupboard just above her,
On tiptoes, reaches up, pulls down
Her new, expensive dressing gown.
So rarely is this piece of nightwear
Taken down from its place of rest,
Though it's the garment she likes best.
It is the kind of thing she might wear
Only if in a certain mood,
Or just to make herself feel good.

2.12

It's creamy white and barely half-length.
Kim lays it out upon the bed;
Her one alternative is calf-length,
And heavy-duty wear instead.
She picks it up and, slowly dressing,
She feels the fabric now caressing
The very contours that she'd mapped;
Her every pore in soft silk wrapped;
A luxury which now enthralls her.
She holds it soft against her face,
Tying it loosely at the waist,
When suddenly a loud voice calls her,
Drawing her from her reverie:
'Hey, Kim, d'you want a cup of tea?'

2.13
She picks the towel up and runs it
Roughly over her matted hair,
Then crosses to the light switch, turns it
Off and goes slowly down the stair.
She sees her husband still reclining,
Looking as though he's been refining
That ancient art of Bacchus' sons:
Drinking from two beer cans at once.
He jumps up; "I'll put on the kettle"
And makes them both a cup of tea.
Kim walks across to the TV,
Turning it off. She grasps the nettle:
'Well, then, since I have been away,
Have you found anything to say?'

2.14
'Yes. Truthfully, I have been thinking
Of things that we could maybe do.
I haven't just been sat here drinking
As you had thought. Well, hadn't you?
But I don't want to cause you sorrow;
I thought we could, perhaps, tomorrow
Enjoy a little trip away:
To Edinburgh for the day.'
She sips some tea before replying.
'Okay. That sounds good. Count me in.'
He smiles. The smile becomes a grin.
Looking at him, she thinks 'He's trying'
And finds herself now smiling back,
Which sends Jim on a different tack.

2.15
Earlier would have been a no-no,
The chance of fun and games tonight,
But seeing her in that silk kimono,
The outlook now was looking bright.
He puts an arm around her shoulder.
She sits, allowing him to hold her.
He says, 'Come up to bed with me.'
She says, 'Shut up and drink your tea.
Let's talk about our expedition
Just now. It's ages since I've been
Out east. It's such a different scene.'
Jim has a sudden premonition:
The trip that Kim is planning now
Won't be the same as his somehow.

2.16
'Some shopping first, before it's busy,
For things to decorate this place.
I'm sorry I got in a tizzy,
But really, it's a pure disgrace.
When was the last time this was painted?
My mum walked in and nearly fainted
When I told her it was ten years.
She hardly could believe her ears.
Now, there's a thought. What about mother?
We'd maybe take her through with us.
She'd help us decorate, no fuss.
Apart from that, there's just one other
Thing I would like, Jim, if I may:
We could be tourists for the day!

2.17
To see the castle at our leisure
And wander down the Royal Mile,
Stopping for tea. Then, for good measure,
Princes Street Gardens for a while.
I'd like to see the new museum;
Onegin's on at The Lyceum;
The Gallery of Modern Art …
Oh, I just don't know where to start.
 'Hang on. I've got to work at seven,
So shopping's really out the game
For me. I'm sorry, it's a shame.
I should be finished by eleven.
We'll have the afternoon to catch
A gallery; a show; a match …'

2.18
'A match? What match? In Edinburgh?
You kept that pretty quiet, mate.
Your planning's obviously thorough.
So, I'm supposed to sit and wait
For you to do your morning's labour
Yet one more time? Do me a favour.
I'm fed up being left alone
While you're at work. You're never home.
You know, your children hardly saw you?
They used to say, 'Mum, who's that guy,
Who stays the night, then says goodbye?'
'That's rubbish.' 'Yes, but it might draw you
Out of this selfish frame of mind.
You used to be so thoughtful, kind.

2.19
'You gave me such consideration.
You couldn't do enough for me.
And I had so much admiration
For how you always tried to be.
But all that's gone. You stand diminished
In my regard. Perhaps we're finished.
It feels there's nothing left to give.
This is no way for us to live.
But do we care enough to sort it?
Can you be bothered thinking through
What needs fixed between me and you?
Or maybe we should just abort it,
And write it off as a lost cause.'
She looks at him with pregnant pause.

2.20
Jim's pallor drains at her suggesting
Their time together's in the past.
He finds it difficult digesting
Her words. His heart is beating fast.
His mouth is dry. His stomach's churning.
He feels a growing passion burning.
Her heart's expression of despair
Has rendered raw emotions bare.
He thinks his lust reciprocated;
Misled by torrents of desire,
He leaps, feet-first, into the mire:
'Kim, love, I think you're just frustrated.
Let's make love till the break of dawn,
Or till my alarm clock comes on.'

2.21
'You hardly need be telepathic
To guess what I am going to say;
My Golden Gate is closed to traffic.
You'll have to find another way
Around the ocean of your ardour.
You'll need to try a good bit harder
To get back into my good books.
Till then, you're stuck with my rebukes;
And though your engine may be burning,
The lock is on your steering wheel.
It's time for you to just get real.
This lady will not be for turning
You on tonight, so think again.'
She pauses briefly, then says, 'Men!

2.22
'Why is it when their passion's rousing
—That place beneath their underpants
Where I am told men's brains have housing —
They'll snap their fingers, think we'll dance
Along to any tune they'll play us;
Be happy that they want to lay us;
Unable to resist their charms,
We'll melt like putty in their arms?
Well, listen. Though your loins are feeling
As if they're primed beef, set to go,
Best of breed at the Highland Show,
And you think yourself so appealing,
Right now, I need you just as much
As automatics need a clutch.'

2.23

She turns and pulls the bean bag from him,
And shoves it full into his face.
His tea, half-drunk, now spills upon him.
Still hot, it falls into the place
His Levis should have been protecting.
His mug across the room projecting,
He jumps up, shouts in scalded pain,
'Oh Jesus Christ! I'm soaked again!
By burning tea! Oh, God Almighty!'
He races up the stair and turns
The shower to cold, to soothe his burns.
'I saw her in that wee silk nightie
And thought the signal green for go.
It wasn't: how was I to know?'

2.24

Two seconds, and the pain's receded.
His pride is hurt, but nothing more.
No hospitalisation needed.
He slinks back down, and in the door.
'Your mug of tea … I didn't mean it,
I'd not have done that if I'd seen it.'
'No harm done, Kim. I know you're right.
We have to talk. We shouldn't fight.
Tomorrow, I'll just take a breather:
No work; no football; just us two;
Do anything you want to do.'
She smiles. 'Okay. No shopping either.
I know how it does in your head.
We'll do some gardening instead.'

Chapter 3

The trees are in their springtime beauty

3.1
The trees are in their springtime beauty.
Jim steps outside and starts the car.
The purchase of a heavy-duty
Battery has improved, by far,
The prospect of the motor starting.
And even though the thought of parting
With extra cash hurt at the time,
It does the job it was designed
To do: i.e. increase the chances
Of getting in to work each day
With minor mishap on the way.
He turns the heater up, then glances
In the wing mirror, checks the gears,
And sits until the windscreen clears.

3.2
It's cold; but then again it would be
At 7:35 a.m.
At least it isn't raining. Could be
A fine day later. One FM
Is blaring loudly from the speakers.
He flicks it on to Two. The Seekers
Carnival is not over yet.
He rummages for a cassette
And finds an eighties' compilation:
Best of the Eagles; Oxygene …
All played to death and back again.
He puts them back and turns the station
To medium wave, Radio 5,
And then reverses out the drive.

3.3
Quite why his wife, at her age, chooses
To tune to One, he doesn't know,
But there it is. She still enthuses
Over the charts and Breakfast Show.
The modern charts: abysmal blunders
From tuneless tarts and one-hit wonders.
Tunes ain't, as far as he can see,
A patch on what they used to be.
This view officially consigns him
To middle age. He gets his hit
Elsewhere, although he won't admit
In public that his youth's behind him.
His zeppelin's showing signs of age:
More potted plant and business page

3.4
Than Bob and Jim. Along the crescent,
Approaches on a paper run
A lone mop-headed adolescent.
Jim stops and shouts across 'Hey, son.
A paper there for number four?'
'No, just the Record for next door.'
'That's fine.' 'But if I havenae got
Them a' delivered, I'll get shot.'
'No sweat. I'll see he gets it after.'
'Right, mister. Dae I get a tip?'
'Aye, on your bike. Less o' your lip.'
The paper boy responds with laughter
And, middle finger firmly raised,
Continues on his round unfazed.

3.5
Jim moves away, furtively glancing
Up at the window of the house,
Where Kim still sleeps. He knows he's chancing
His arm, going out to work. A mouse
In carpet slippers couldn't rival
His silent exit. Kim's revival
From alcoholic dormancy
Was likely to be hours away.
And so he'd left her soundly sleeping,
Excusing his recalcitrance
On mitigating circumstance.
He thought his promise freed from keeping
—The one to stay at home and talk —
And if he landed in the dock,

3.6
With Kim the judge and Kim the jury,
With Kim the clerkess of the court,
Facing the force of female fury,
Without a friend to lend support,
He'd have the charges all refuted
Before the sentence was commuted.
'M'lady, I am innocent.
My promise was sincerely meant.
I woke this morning, hale and hearty,
Prepared to join in full debate
Regarding our collective fate,
But you did choose not to be party
To such discourse; you slept right through
My best endeavours to wake you.

3.7

'The charges, therefore, are unproven,
And I considered off the hook.
Such travesty, as has been woven
Before this court, makes me no crook.'
Thus his defence is formulated,
The prosecution case deflated.
A whiff of guilt, however, hangs
Around his arguments. Some pangs
Of conscience flare deep down, internal,
Perplexing; for if truth be told,
His actions were not quite so bold.
Fearing another damned infernal
Heart to heart, being just a bloke,
He'd gone AWOL before she woke.

3.8

Such heart-to-hearts are never really
The kind of thing he likes to do.
The prospect of a touchy-feely
Encounter gave him reason to
Be busy in another matter.
Quite happy to just sit and natter
To anyone who comes his way,
To chew the fat, pass time of day
In amiable conversation,
To talk — spelled with capital 'T' —
Spelled 't-r-o-u-b-l-e'.
And this was such a situation.
So, bedroom curtains still drawn tight,
He disappears from view. First right,

3.9

Then left down Neilston Road, proceeding
Behind the abbey, through the town,
He takes the one-way system, leading
To Arkleston, and turns on down
To the M8, accelerating.
At once, he finds himself berating
A Mini in the middle lane
At 50 miles an hour. In vain,
He curses this well-known manoeuvre,
And wishes other folk could be
As thoughtful on the road as he.
And knowing not a thing would move her
From chosen path, decides to pass.
He pulls out, hears a sudden blast

3.10

From someone's horn behind him; braking,
A large Toyota's on his tail;
In the red mist of his own making,
He hadn't seen the vapour trail.
He moves back in. It passes sleekly,
Glowering back at Jim, who meekly
Stares straight ahead and drops his speed,
Apologising for the deed.
He sits behind the Mini's fender,
Then moments later takes the ramp
That leads off to the Luma Lamp,
Restored to 30s' Deco splendour.
The fifty pitches seem bereft,
With only just a handful left,

3.11
Of youthful hope and aspiration;
Hard-pressed by progress, built upon,
The playing fields of generations
Were shrunken now and almost gone.
We, in our keenness to develop,
Each day unwittingly envelop
In concrete, girders, steel and tar
A little more of who we are.
Shared histories, which guide and mould us
Are worn away: the threads that run
Unseen from father down to son,
Whose woven intricacies hold us
In tightly-knit communities,
And help shape our identities,

3.12
Unravel slowly down the ages;
At best, recorded in a book
Upon a shelf, with faded pages,
In which no one will ever look.
Off Shieldhall Road, he slows down, nearing
Ardneil Arduthie Engineering,
Now trading as a lesser link
Of A-Zee Multi-Something Inc.
Joe, of a certain generation,
Past being trend, or market-led,
Insists on calling it 'A-Zed',
And won't admit the corporation,
Whom he now owes employment to,
Is different from the people who

3.13

Collect the bins and run the buses,
And chase folk for their rent arrears.
He doesn't know what all the fuss is;
His job's not changed in thirty years.
Back then, as now, a job requiring
A time-served sparky for the wiring,
Required a sparky, should we be
Ltd., Inc. or plc.
Ardneil, when he was in his heyday,
Made sure the job was done on time.
If not, your job was on the line;
Your pocket would be light by payday.
Hard as a rock, abrasive, rude,
You always knew just where you stood

3.14

With old Ardneil and his co-founder,
Arduthie. Things were good for years.
Recession saw the business flounder,
And slowly fall about their ears.
Arduthie drank; Ardneil took solace
Within the arms of Mrs. Wallace,
A local girl who did the books,
Whose head for figures — and good looks —
Prompted the offer of employment.
Her husband often worked away;
Three nights a week, the pair would stay
Behind to seek covert enjoyment;
While their libidos ran amok,
The business found itself in hock.

3.15

It all came to a sticky ending:
The nephew of a neighbour, who
Had gossiped to a woman bending
The ear of someone else she knew,
Who'd told a mate, who'd told his missus
Of secret trysts and furtive kisses,
Had spoken at the social club
To someone who'd been at the pub,
Who knew a long-time friend of Mr.
Wallace's next-door neighbour's son,
Who'd long been having carnal fun
With Mr. Wallace's wee sister.
The word was out. A trap was set,
Although they didn't know it yet.

3.16

They caught the couple in flagrante;
Ardneil, atop his desk, quite bare;
His paramour in bra and panties.
Wallace calmly approached the pair.
'My wife. I've just come to collect her.
Please know I am a tax inspector.'
The auditors were in next day,
Ardneil, Arduthie led away,
Replaced in course by the receiver.
Cut off, without a dialling tone,
The firm had ceased to be their own.
And Mrs. Wallace? He did leave her.
Word is, she now spends winter nights
At peace among the Carmelites.

3.17

'Ach, Joe, that tale is getting taller
Each time you choose to give it air.'
'Jim! Must be you that's getting smaller.
I didn't see you standing there.'
Inside, the squad's begun to gather,
The boss already in a lather
As he confronts his biggest fear:
The end of the financial year.
Headhunted from a city rival,
McKay — mid-thirties, family man,
Wife, 2.4 kids, caravan —
Had engineered a big revival
In fortunes since he had appeared.
The heavy losses that were feared

3.18

Had turned round; the firm saved from closing.
Ambitious, now with rising stock,
The corporate style he was imposing
Was something of a culture shock,
However, to the longest serving
Workers, who with, at times unswerving
Resistance to the latest creed,
Had caused his hairline to recede.
His best attempts at group conversion,
With mission statements, values, aims,
And challenging team-building games,
Regarded as a mild diversion;
Industrial and clerical
Alike saw evangelical

3.19
Attempts to preach of business saviours,
Of profit motives, his benign
Attempts to alter base behaviour,
Awareness of the bottom line,
To give the workforce clearer focus,
As merely high-flown hocus-pocus;
Just jargon from across the pond
That's here today, tomorrow gone.
McKay believed it resolutely,
With all the fervent zeal of men
Who've seen the light, who're born again,
Trusting its power absolutely.
But not its power to do the books;
That task required specialist cooks.

3.20
He paces up and down with mounting
Anxiety, watching the clock.
'Procedure for year-end accounting.
Right, Jim, we have to count the stock.'
'Yes. Joe, and when he gets here, Gary
Will get a fix on what we carry.'
'Receipts and issues to go through?
Outstanding invoices?' 'That's Pru.'
'Customers' bills prepared and costed?'
'Yep, all okay and up to date.
Wee Sandra has been working late
Each night this month. The girl's exhausted.'
'And follow-up?' 'Debtors are low,
As hopefully the books will show.'

3.21

He reads the list until completed,
Then says to Jim, 'What will I do
To help?' Expletives here deleted,
Jim thinks 'Just stay well out of view',
But says 'There's nothing too essential
That needs a man of your credentials.
As long as you're around, that's all.
If need be, I'll give you a call.'
They nod, in ritual concordance,
Respectful of each other's role.
He goes and checks his pigeon hole
For any new head office ordinance.
Gary appears. He gives a gruff
'Morning.' The boy sounds pretty rough.

3.22

A fact not lost on Joe who, straightways,
Has Gary working up a sweat
In punishment (and cure) for late ways.
There's little likelihood he'll get
An Alka Seltzer, tea or Beecham's.
There's tried and tested ways to teach them.
The kid, still wet behind the ears,
Will benefit from all Joe's years
Of heavy nights and mornings after.
Apprenticed for just seven weeks,
He's hardly out of baby breeks.
But if he turns out half the grafter
That Joe has been, he'll do okay.
If he can just survive the day …

3.23

Jim leaves them counting drums of cable.
Joe sits and watches with a cup
Of tea, as Gary, barely able
To stand, attempts to measure up.
Inside the office, Pru's rebooting
The system, and soon starts inputting
Receipts and issues, one by one,
While Jim sorts out the ledger run.
'How's John? Has he been keeping better?'
Jim stops and says, 'I think he's fine.
I don't think he can find the time
To phone these days. As for a letter,
The thought would give him writer's cramp;
He'd need a mortgage for the stamp.'

3.24

'And Kate?' 'Och, aye, unlike her brother,
She's on the phone ten times a week.
She seems much closer to her mother;
The pair of them know how to speak.
And your lot?' 'Fine, young Ann's at college.
July she's finished. All that knowledge
Of business studies and finance,
I hope it gives the girl a chance
Of finding work on qualifying.
I meant to ask, d'you think Mckay
Might take her on?' 'I don't see why
He couldn't. There's no harm in trying.
Ask him once the year-end is by.
He's quite a reasonable guy.'

3.25
They work on, interrupted only
Each fifteen minutes by McKay.
Perhaps he feels a little lonely;
More likely wants to keep an eye
On things; year-end's a heavy onus,
Especially when there's a bonus
To think about, dependent on
The figures they're at work upon.
It makes the morning's work more stressful
To have a boss with worker ants
Marching around his underpants.
By noon, their efforts are successful.
The paperwork input and filed,
The stock returns all reconciled.

3.26
Jim fills his spreadsheet; first with debits
Summating to the business costs;
And, in another column, credits;
Then calculates the profit/loss
For all the projects now completed,
Accruing income unreceipted,
Plus other miscellaneous
—Though some would say nefarious —
Deliberations. First impressions
Are positive. He'd place a bet
That forecast out-turns will be met,
Which might persuade McKay's expression
To lighten up, relax a bit,
As targets look like being hit.

3.27
He's busy on the phone, however;
His body language says 'keep clear'.
The others stand around and blether,
Wondering if they need be here,
Till Joe announces that he's making
Tracks; with a thirst in need of slaking.
He says to Gary, 'Come on, son,
It's time to go. I'll buy you one.'
They say their brief goodbyes and shuffle
Off out the door, get in Joe's car,
And head towards the nearest bar.
Inside, a closed door fails to muffle
The sound of argument within.
An uncharacteristic din,

3.28
Beyond the sound of idle chatter.
Jim turns to Pru. 'Away you go.
I'll stay and find out what's the matter.
Probably you won't want to know.'
'Okay, I will, with your permission.
I must admit I've no ambition
To be on the receiving end
Of what's upset our mutual friend.
I'll see you Monday. Leave you to it.'
Jim turns and walks across the floor,
Knocks loudly on the boss's door,
Pushes it open, walks in through it
And says, 'Boss, that's us finished here.
Results are looking good this year'.

3.29

'Fuck the results.' Jim stands, astonished
At what he's now subjected to,
As never having been admonished
For helping guide the business through
Financial year-end machinations,
Associated tribulations
Included, he is at a loss
Why, up to now, a decent boss,
Should turn on him with such malicious
Response to simply stated fact.
That didn't warrant being attacked.
It's not his nature to be vicious.
Jim stands his ground and asks him, 'Why?'
A minute passes, then McKay

3.30

Turns round to Jim and says 'I'm sorry.
Uncalled for, Jim. I didn't mean
To sound like that … derogatory
Towards the efforts of the team.
Their efforts are appreciated.
Each one of them is highly rated.
Oh God, I'm sounding like a clown.
I'm worried they might close us down.
Don't say a thing. It's confidential:
Restructuring is under way
Across the whole of the UK.
They say they have to take essential
Cost-cutting measures to survive,
Or else the company won't thrive.'

3.31
They stand in silent rumination
Attempting to digest the news.
'What possible justification
Could anyone have to excuse
A call of such inanity?
Closure would be insanity.
Someone, somewhere, made a mistake.
It can't be right. For any sake,
We turn in profits. You just told me.'
Jim nods assent. 'Well, if that's so,
We'll be all right. They're bound to know.
I'll phone Head Office. They can't hold me
Responsible. I've turned a loss
Into a profit; cut the costs.'

3.32
The volume of his protestation
Increases slowly, as if to
Convince himself their situation
Is strong enough to see them through.
But, now a veteran campaigner,
Jim sees it all a little plainer;
He's seen and heard all this before.
It doesn't faze him anymore.
He meets, with stoical dispassion,
The prospect of a further change.
'That's management: to rearrange
The business in whatever fashion
Is popular at business school …
And that's downsizing, as a rule.'

3.33

'Your attitude does you no credit,
It's cynical. I don't approve.
I really wish you hadn't said it.
You don't have anything to prove
To me, but think on future prospects;
Participation in new projects.
Change can be beneficial too,
And opportunities are few
And far enough between to throw your
Future away with such displays.
Such criticism rarely pays.
You've been here long enough to know you're
In with the bricks, part of the plan,
A fully-fledged company man.

3.34

The company will not forsake you;
It looks after its favoured sons.
Show them you're willing and they'll make you
Secure, one of the chosen ones.
No need to be a doubting Thomas.
We'll see you all right, Jim. I promise.'
Such optimism is naïve,
Thinks Jim. He really does believe
What he just said. A little nervous
At the implicit threat contained,
Jim says, 'So what is to be gained?
Year after year of loyal service;
Long hours of working night and day;
Missing your children grow and play,

3.35
Your partner lonely, unforgiving;
And all for what? More of the same?'
'You and the rest earn a good living
Working here. It's unfair to blame
Domestic woes on your employer.
I don't think you could find a lawyer
Smart enough to make that one stick,
Old son.' The condescending prick!
'You think your faith gives you protection,
Salvation from the dreaded dole,
Exemption from the begging bowl?
Your narrow-minded introspection
Is, at this moment, needed least.
It's not the nature of the beast

3.36
To undertake the role of carer;
The leopard cannot change its spot.
And while you couldn't have been fairer,
Personally, to me, it's not
In any way obligatory
That I condone such predatory
Intentions, even though we know
It's pointless fighting. What of Joe?
At his age, he's beyond retraining.
D'you think he'll ever work again?
I doubt it very much. And then
There's Gary. Will you be explaining
To him why his time won't be served?
The lad's done well, and he's deserved

3.37
Better than this. And all the others;
Their livelihoods taken away?
How many husbands, fathers, mothers
With mouths to feed and bills to pay?
There'll be no job, then, for Pru's daughter?
The bairn's flung out with the bath water.
The consequences that ensue
Affect our children's future too,
With less apprenticeships to enter,
Less of a chance to earn a skill,
Just low-paid service jobs to fill.
And those who constitute the centre
Drop off, see it reduce in size
And old divides repolarize.'

3.38
'You're talking like a politician
Or union rep. The days are gone
When socialism held a position
Of influence. Times have moved on
Since then. It's a new situation.'
'I don't have an affiliation
To any party, left or right,
Or in between, that's not my fight;
But when we find ourselves maltreated
And dumped upon, with scant respect,
It doesn't take much intellect
To know discussion may be heated.
What's happening just isn't right.
We can't give up without a fight.

3.39
'There's plenty work to keep us going;
But someone needs to have the will.'
'Okay, but we've no way of knowing
How lies the bigger picture, still
Less how we're faring in the global
Marketplace; and your thoughts, though noble,
Miss the reality: there may
Be casualties along the way.
But if the company's well-being
Is guaranteed, the greater good
Is served. However, if we stood
Still, we would very soon be seeing
The competition put us out
Of business, Jim … of that, no doubt.

3.40
'Think of a race. To be a winner,
You must be lean and fit. If not,
You lose. So we have to get thinner,
Reduce the overheads we've got.'
'Such allegories are simplistic.
And anyway, it's optimistic
To try to win a race, God knows,
By cutting off your bloody toes!
What athlete doesn't thrive on muscles?
They don't get thin and fade away,
They build, by exercise, each day.
A strong heart, vigorous corpuscles,
And willing lungs all join to bring
Fitness and health. Another thing:

3.41
'It's not a race. The founder's vision,
Set down in stone, by all agreed —
'To make a living, by provision
Of services, where there's a need' —
Is just as relevant as ever.
Your mission statements may sound clever,
But that old chestnut does define
Why we exist. The bottom line
Is — should be — people.' 'Jim, come off it!
You've been around the block enough
Not to believe in all that guff.
You know the bottom line is profit;
Purely and simply down to cash;
The rest is all just balderdash.'

3.42
'That whole philosophy's immoral.'
'Morality won't pay your bills.
Look, really, I don't want to quarrel.
We can't, between us, solve the ills
Of modern living, but survival
Is preferable to a rival
Taking us over. You'd agree?'
'No, I would not. I fail to see
What difference changes at board level
Would mean to those of us now faced
Without a job. We're still displaced.
It's no concern of mine who revel
In playing the boardroom power game.
Self-preservation seems the aim.'

3.43
'Yes, for us all: self-preservation …'
He pauses, then picks up his keys.
'Jim, can you treat this conversation
As purely confidential, please?
No need to cause undue disquiet,
Or generate a ruddy riot.
It might not happen anyway.
And, if it does, it's months away.'
Jim stands in silent contemplation,
As if he's lost the will to fight.
McKay turns round, flicks off the light.
'Jim, we've no cause for confrontation.
Buy you some lunch?' But Jim says 'No.
I'll get my jacket and just go.'

3.44
They shut the door and, walking over
The yard towards their cars, McKay
Flicks the remote, unlocks his Rover,
And nods to Jim a curt goodbye.
Jim watches him accelerating
Off up the road, then indicating
Before the junction, turning right,
And disappearing out of sight.
He puts the key in the ignition
And turns. The engine doesn't start,
And he, unable to depart,
Slumps forward in abject submission,
And sits awhile in sunken pose
While round him wash his worldly woes.

3.45

What next? I'll likely have a puncture,
He thinks with self-indulgent sigh.
Called to account, I, at this juncture,
Could neither square, nor certify,
My balance sheet: it's out of kilter.
My engine needs a new oil filter;
My spark plug's spluttered to a stop;
My petrol gauge shows not a drop.
My asset base is stripped and crumbling:
The kids have grown up now and gone;
Friends, scattered round the globe, moved on;
My job and marriage prospects tumbling.
Years of investment, just to see
One liability: that's me.

3.46

But soon enough, the clouds are shifting,
Pierced by his mobile's ringing tone.
'Dad? John.' He finds his spirits lifting.
'I've got no credit on my phone.
Just let you know, be home tomorrow,
Okay?' 'Yes, yes. D'you need to borrow
Cash to get here?' 'No, no, I'm fine.
Speak to you soon.' At that, the line
Goes dead. He steps out, lifts the bonnet,
And rakes about with who knows what,
—   A car mechanic he is not —
Then spies a bus and clambers on it,
Abandoning his cheerless gloom
Inside his broken-down saloon.

Chapter 4

Kim's rudely wakened from her slumber

4.1

Kim's rudely wakened from her slumber
By ringing on the telephone
Downstairs. 'Who's dialling our number
This time of day? We're not at home.
My head is sore. My eyes are bleary.
My poor old body's tired and weary.'
She pulls the duvet round her head
And snuggles back into the bed.
Two minutes pass. The sound of ringing
Echoes around the house again.
She lifts her head. It's five past ten.
She curses, sits upright, and swinging
Her legs round, steps on to the floor
And stumbles over to the door.

4.2

The answerphone kicks into action.
'Hi, Kim here. 'Fraid there's no one home.
If you wish verbal interaction,
Please leave your name after the tone,
Unless you want to sell a kitchen:
Don't bother trying to put your pitch in,
We've got one; and we're double-glazed.
Such messages will be erased.'
Beep. 'Mum, it's me. Are you still sleeping?
I can't wait. I'm off into town.
Just let you know, I'm coming down
Tomorrow, sometime. Hope you're keeping
Fine. I've some news that just won't keep.
See you tomorrow. Bye.' Click. Beep.

4.3

Kim hears her daughter's voice and hurries
Downstairs, arriving just too late.
She hears the message and now worries
What news there is that just can't wait.
She's fallen pregnant; or miscarried;
She's got engaged; or getting married;
She's dropping out; or got the sack;
She's homesick and she's moving back;
Health problems. Kate, what ills afflict you?
She lifts the handset, tries to call:
No answer. Then her mobile. All
She hears is, 'Sorry, can't connect you.
The mobile you are trying to reach
May be switched off.' How we beseech

4.4

Our children, as their independence
Grows steadily through teenage years,
To keep in touch. With scant attendance
To primitive parental fears,
They condescend to give sporadic
Bulletins as to their nomadic,
Nocturnal, gallivanting traipse
Through hormones, highs and hair-brained scrapes …
If we're in luck, that is. We're grateful
For any microscopic scraps
Of news that fall into our laps,
Devouring titbits by the plateful.
And thus is our umbilical
Discord, in metaphysical

4.5
Terms, eased. Right now the plate, however,
Is empty, and she'll have to wait
For information. Not too clever
To have you mobile switched off, Kate.
Are you just coming down for dinner?
I hope you aren't any thinner;
Last time you seemed to have lost weight.
You kids just don't appreciate
The benefits of proper cooking,
Of fruit and veg and plenty greens,
Regular roughage, bran and beans.
Convenience food has you all looking
Malnourished, underweight and thin.
I'll get a big food shopping in;

4.6
I'll make some broth; I'll do some baking;
We'll have a roast with Yorkshire pud.
And thus tomorrow's undertaking
Is planned, though at the thought of food,
Kim's hangover affirms its presence.
She groans in feeble acquiescence
And, reaching down into her bag,
Lights up a surreptitious fag.
She draws it deep, feels a delicious
Frisson of pleasure, then exhales.
This secret vice her partner fails
To comprehend. To him, pernicious,
Cancerous, costly. Never fear,
For at the moment, he's not here!

4.7

Now, there's a point. He made a solemn
Promise to be with me today.
He'll be at work. I think I'll call him.
Oh, what's the use? And anyway,
I'd rather have a long, hot shower
Before these dull aches overpower
My will to live. Or else a cup
Of coffee, just to perk me up.
She takes her coffee upstairs, showers,
And dressing in her oldest clothes,
Refreshed, if not recovered, goes
To Kate's old room. 'I'll get some flowers;
The room is looking pretty bare,
Un-lived-in; and it needs some air.

4.8

And so do I.' Pathetic, sickly,
Foreswearing ever to be drunk
Again, she looks around. How quickly
We gather such assorted junk:
An ancient wooden-shafted putter;
Replacement piece of plastic gutter;
A broken clock; some plastic bags
Filled up with old clothes, sheets and rags;
A knitting machine from the twenties.
All useless, to be thrown away,
But kept for use some rainy day.
She sets to work and quickly empties
The temporary rubbish store,
Moving it to John's room, next door.

4.9

She dusts and hoovers; pulls the bed down
To give it air; puts on fresh sheets.
She thinks she'll maybe put her head down,
Just for a while. Her eye, though, meets
A tiny corner of offending
Wallpaper, loose and needing mending.
To bring about a swift repair,
She pulls at it and makes a tear
That reaches almost to the ceiling.
'Shit!' she exclaims, as in her hands,
The gap upon the wall expands.
'Oh well, I'd better keep on peeling.
Too late to stop now, I suppose.'
She rips at each piece now exposed

4.10

And with the aid of sponge and scraper,
Within an hour, the bedroom walls
Are pretty much devoid of paper,
Which, by the time she's finished, sprawls
Across the room she'd been spring-cleaning
An hour or so beforehand, meaning
She has to clear it all again.
She fills some black bin liners, then
Sticks them next door as well. Delighted
By all she's done, she thinks to take
A well-deserved and needed break.
The morning mail has now alighted
Upon the mat. She lifts the pile.
One postmark brings a knowing smile.

4.11
She recognises Shona's writing,
The tiny, flowing, backhand script
She's used throughout the years, delighting
Kim with its fun and warmth and wit,
Though seeming smaller as time passes.
Kim's maybe needing reading glasses?
Or Shona just has less to say
Than she had in a former day?
Back through the house, she boils the kettle
And makes herself a cup of tea.
Out in the garden, she can see
The sun out. She decides to settle
Down on the back doorstep to tend
The letter from her oldest friend.

4.12
'Dear Kim. Hola! How are you doing?
I hope you're fine. And Jim, how's he?
Young Katie, is she still pursuing
Her childhood dream? And John, he'll be
Twenty this year? God, I remember
When he was born; first of September;
Pouring with rain; at Rottenrow,
His tiny little face aglow
With life; and you just out of labour;
Knackered from sixteen hours in there,
Wanting a brush to fix your hair!
Where's the time gone? Do me a favour:
Send me a photograph of Kate
And John ... anything up to date,

4.13
To show me how the pair have grown up.
John was the image of your dad.
Anyway, Kim, I have to own up,
Things down here have been pretty bad.
You'll see above that my address is
Different. And what I must confess is
That Pete and I have finished. Split.
For good. Twenty-one years. That's it!
I write this, but I can't believe it,
Though we've been separated now
Since New Year; and I don't know how
We take a lifetime and just heave it
Out with the garbage, and expect
Life to go on, with no effect.

4.14
My adult years have all been with him;
Not just my lover, but my friend.
But now my heart beats without rhythm.
I can't write more. I have to end.'
The words break off. The revelation
Fills Kim with shock, then consternation;
She turns the page; 'It's me again.
I'm sorry, Kim, to be a pain.
I've really had no one to talk to.
To see my feelings written down …
I took a taxi into town,
Got out, decided then to walk to
The sea front, where I've been all day,
Thinking of what I want to say.

4.15

I have a flat; a good location,
Quite central; smaller than before,
Of course, but the accommodation
Will do for now. We're second floor.
Josh is with me; he sees his father
At weekends, though I think he'd rather
Be with his mates. Poor Josh. He copes
So well with his parental dopes
And their increasing useless presence.
He's grown into a fine young man.
He's fluent now in Catalan.
You knew Pete got him sailing lessons
When we first came? The silly goat
Thought Catalan a twin-hulled boat.

4.16

'He's hurting, but he doesn't show it.
Typical Josh, he doesn't say.
I love him, and need him to know it.
I'm there for him both night and day;
I give him hugs to help him through it.
He humours me and lets me do it.
I'm not sure who's supporting who.
Oh, Kim, I'm not sure why we do
The things we do. I hear you asking
What happened to tear us apart?
What happened to this brave new start
Of ours? We should have been here, basking
In all the pleasures of the Med,
But look at where we are instead.

4.17

'For ages now, I've been so lonely.
Pete's working all his waking hours,
He's been promoted now. If only
He'd given to this life of ours
The same, wholehearted application
As he did to his occupation,
Things maybe would be different now.
In due course, we began to row;
Soon, everything was a potential
Argument. In particular,
There were extra-curricular
Activities he deemed essential
To building healthy team morale.
At least, that was the rationale.

4.18

'A team works when a team's united'
Was one phrase from his repertoire.
Staff outings — partners not invited —
Began as trips to tapas bars.
Predictably, inebriation
Soon brought about an escalation
To full-blown nights out on the town.
Some mornings, I would come around
To find his side had not been slept in.
I turned into an angry, sad,
Suspicious battleaxe, half-mad.
It's so degrading to be kept in
The dark. When quizzed, he'd just avoid
My eyes, and call me paranoid.

4.19
Some little tart at work — Luisa —
Invariably figured in
What little he did tell me. She's a
Secretary; blonde, twenties, thin.
He'd say, "Just your imagination
Run wild". Who knows? In resignation,
I built a life all of my own,
Quite separate from the one we'd known.
I'd kept up both my language classes.
This guy — Jari, a Dutchman — had
Us back to his bachelor pad
One evening, just for a few glasses
Of Tempranillo. He was fun,
Good-looking, though a little young

4.20
For girls like us. But then, on leaving,
He whispered in my ear, 'Please stay.
Unless my eyes have been deceiving
Me, you are so sad. Why this way?'
I fled from his apartment, fearful
Of his approach. Later, my tearful
State wakened Josh during the night.
He asked me. "Mum, are you all right?"
I don't recall what lies I told him.
It's funny how one person's lies
Draw veils over so many eyes.
Just happy he was there, to hold him,
I told him I was fine and said.
"It's nothing, Josh, go back to bed".

4.21

'The next few days, my head was spinning.
I cried for hours; a dam had burst.
Defences that were underpinning
My fragile state had turned to dust.
I stopped the classes, but the tutor
Brought up my file on his computer,
And gave Jari my home address.
He turned up here. I was a mess.
"I didn't come to see your make-up",
Was his response to protests that
I wasn't fit for tea and chat.
He then said, "Shona, will you take up
The offer of a coffee, tea,
Or any other drink with me?

4.22

"But, if I am unwelcome, say it.
Just tell me: Go away! Depart!
And if you do, I shall obey it,
Though I shall go with heavy heart".
I found myself in fits of laughter
At his theatrics. In truth, after
So long in such a sad old place,
He'd brought a smile back to my face.
I know it wasn't very clever,
But, Josh with Pete, off down the coast,
I asked him in. It was the most
Ridiculous decision ever.
We talked for hours; he was the spark
That brought me from that lonely, dark

4.23
'Place I had been; and when the talking
Had stopped, I stood up, took his hand
—I hope you don't find this too shocking;
I pray, Kim, you will understand–
Through to the bedroom; there, undressing
In silence; slowly there caressing
Each other, lightly, where we stood.
Then to my bed. His aptitude
Belied his years. Without direction,
He made love to me in a way
I cherish to this very day:
With such desire, composed affection,
That Pete and I shared in the past,
But, sadly, didn't seem to last.

4.24
'We met again that week, on Thursday,
This time at his place. It was just
As wonderful as on the first day.
I felt alive again. Pete must
Have noticed something, been suspicious.
I couldn't care. The whole, delicious
Scenario had knocked my brain
On to a wholly different plane.
But soon my good old Presbyterian
Upbringing kicked into top gear.
The 'G' word started to appear.
I'd thought myself mature, Iberian,
But found, the longer things went on,
Less joy came from the liaison.

4.25

'Guilt. Is it ours, or universal?
Was it invented by John Knox?
Its silent, sleekit, sly dispersal
Creeps up on you like chicken pox.
A rectifier of behaviour,
It points us all towards our saviour.
Oh God, I find myself still full
Of all I learned in Sunday school.
I tried to finish it with Jari,
But he was devastated; said
He'd rather be a monk, instead,
And, wait for it, asked if I'd marry
Him. Marry him? The silly lump
Was well and truly off his chump.

4.26

'Hormones, endorphins, they're not truthful.
They lead us up such garden paths.
In mazes, lost, a million youthful
Souls wander in the aftermaths
Of love's young dreams in tragic tatters.
But not that any of this matters.
Poor Jari couldn't face the fact
That, as my lover, he'd been sacked.
He came up to the house, quite blazing,
And challenged Pete to have a fight.
When he heard why, Pete punched his lights
Out, then sat down. It was amazing:
I thought he'd do the same to me,
But we just talked. I cried, as he

4.27
Did too, hurt by my indiscretion.
The fences keeping us apart
Began to fall. My full confession
Assuaged my guilty, heavy heart.
We talked in frank and honest fashion,
Seeking the reasons that our passion
Had turned to poisonous despair.
Out of the blue, he took me, there.
My heart beat fast; his hands were trembling;
He made love like a man consumed
By grief and loss, to find exhumed
A lifeless corpse, decayed, dissembling.
He gave a shudder as he came,
Tearfully whispering my name.

4.28
'He'd packed his bags and gone by morning.
I don't think he could bear my face.
Just upped and left me without warning.
Of course, we had to sell the place.
And thus I am where you now find me.
To this apartment, fate's assigned me.
I have two cats – Janet and Ed –
Who keep me company instead.
And Jari? He went back to Holland.
I think the poor lad got cold feet,
Shit-scared of running into Pete.
I want Pete back. I've tried to call him,
But I don't get too much respect
From him right now. I don't expect

4.29

'An evening filled with wine and roses,
But it would just be nice to talk.
I think he needs it, but he closes
His mind to me, and tries to block
The whole thing out. Well, now I'm finished.
I hope I don't stand too diminished
In your eyes. How I miss my mum
To talk to. Kim, will you please come
Out soon? I'll meet you at Girona.
Stay a few days; a week; or more.
I promise I won't be a bore.
My love to all. Your old friend, Shona.
P.S. It's twenty-one degrees,
So leave behind your anti-freeze.'

4.30

Kim puts the last page on the table
Beside the others, stupefied
By what she's read. She's hardly able
To take it in; quite mystified
By their old friends' bizarre proceedings,
She gives the letter two more readings
To check she fully understood;
That nothing had been misconstrued.
But, no; the sorry tale's related
In full a second time, and then,
In full, it all unfolds again.
'Oh, what a mess they've procreated,'
She sighs with undisguised despair.
'I wish, for her sake, I was there.'

4.31
She gets up from the doorstep, needing
A breath of air to clear her head.
The cat, sat on the mat, needs feeding;
She pours some milk; 'They've made their bed,
They'll have to lie in it — though lying,
Root cause of such unedifying
Denouement, not perhaps the most
Appropriate way to signpost
Their matrimonial disaster.
She steps outside, and starts to pick
At weeds and dead leaves, lying thick
Around the old cotoneaster
Beside the back door. She reflects
On Shona, Pete; how love and sex

4.32
Make fools of us and our intentions;
Fools who rush blindly, unconstrained;
Fools paralysed by guilt's subventions;
Whose passionate expression chained,
Creates in us such fraught and fretful
Frustrations. We play out, regretful,
A haunted and recurring scene,
Reprising roles that might have been.
With single-minded application,
She works along the flower bed
And round the corner, by the shed,
Removing the accumulation
Of fallen leaves and scattered twigs
Bare-handed. Then, with spade, she digs

4.33
The border earth from top to bottom,
Lifting and turning, breaking down
The hard-pressed earth that's lain since autumn.
She slows, carefully walking round
The shoots of daffodils and other
New springtime blooms now breaking cover.
That done, she steps down on the lawn.
Uncultivated, played-upon
For years, its unkempt, threadbare patches
Anger her suddenly. Worn holes
Around imaginary goals
Where John had played out football matches,
Are dug out. One by one, each lump
Is piled in an unsightly dump

4.34
Beyond the path; then, any traces
Of moss and weed soon follow, too.
The edging, overgrown in places,
Is cut right back. She stops to view
The end result of her excision,
At once regretting the decision
To operate. For now, alas,
There are more holes than there is grass.
'Oh dear.' Her garden's dire appearance
Is even worse, now, than it was.
But she, with just the merest pause,
Impulsively completes the clearance,
Until there's not a hint of green
Remaining where the lawn had been.

4.35
She leaves the debris. Jim can clear it
This afternoon, when he gets home.
The doorbell rings. She doesn't hear it.
For, in a world all of her own,
This new space with design potential
Has caused the bulk of Kim's essential
Functions to momentarily
Close down. She's temporarily
Off-message, incommunicado.
Creative juices, it appears,
Have caused malfunction of her ears.
Sight of herbaceous Eldorado
Has rendered her oblivious
To matters multifarious,

4.36
Particularly to the figure
Now sitting on the garden wall
Out front, who, with respectful vigour,
Had rung and rung, and tried to call …
To no avail. So, he's concluded,
Naturally, he's been excluded
Due to the fact that no one's home.
And rather than get up and roam
Around the neighbourhood in aimless
Fashion, he'd sit and catch some rays.
Around the corner, Jim's keen gaze
Spots someone by his house, yet nameless,
Till, moving further up the street,
He cottons on. 'Good grief: It's Pete!'

4.37

He calls out 'Pete!' Pete turns round grinning.
'Jimbo!' 'What are you doing here?'
'Just came to see if Saints are winning!
And it's your turn to buy the beer!'
'Fat chance of that.' 'Of what?' 'Of either!
I'd put my hard-earned cash on neither!'
They laugh, shake hands; 'No joking, though,
If you're not busy, we could go
To Tynecastle to see the footy.'
'The Nou Camp hasn't got a game?'
'Well, aye, but it's just not the same.
A Buddie's got to do his duty.
I need to hear the kick and thud
Of boot on leather in the mud.

4.38

'Last week was Barca–Celta Vigo;
4–1; Rivaldo, Kluivert (3).
Two weeks beforehand, Deportivo.'
'Sure doesn't sound the same to me.
I'm up for it. Come in; two seconds;'
He turns to go inside and beckons
His friend to follow. 'Kim! You home?'
'I'm out here, and I've got a bone
To pick with you. You left me sleeping.'
'I'm sorry. I apologise.
But look who's here. What a surprise!
Come in, Pete.' 'Hi, Kim. How you keeping?'
'Pete! Long time no see. How are you?
And how's Luisa? She fine too?'

Chapter 5

Some temporary leave is granted

5.1
4.35 p.m. Bewailing
The fact they've missed the game, both Pete
And Jim are sick and tired of trailing
Around the shops on Princes Street.
Sensing the duo disenchanted,
Some temporary leave is granted,
But with conditions: 'Don't go far,
Or disappear into a bar.
The pair of you are in hot water.
If I come back and you're not here,
Your lives won't be worth living. Clear?
I won't be long. Let's say a quarter
Past five. We'll meet across the street
Beside that statue; by that seat.'

5.2
Accepting meekly Kim's restrictions,
They turn and make their way across
The road, out of her jurisdiction,
And sit down. 'So: Kim's still the boss!'
Jim looks at Pete. Pete sits there, grinning.
'And always was, from the beginning.
At least, I give her that belief,
Though she has cause to give me grief.
But what the hell's your misdemeanour?
I thought that she'd be pleased to see
You. Her reaction was, to me,
A total shock. I haven't seen her
As angry since … well, since last night,
In actual fact. Perhaps you might

5.3
'Enlighten me as to the detail?
And who the hell's Luisa, Pete?'
'Oh, Kim will be okay. Some retail
Therapy will reduce the heat
On you. It's me she wants to string up.
It didn't take her long to bring up
Our situation. From her tone,
I take it she's been on the phone
To Shona?' 'Not that I'm aware of.
What's happened?' 'Really? You don't know?'
'I don't.' 'Honestly?' 'Jesus, No!'
'Right, well, it looks as though the pair of
Them have me tried, convicted, hung,
Boil-washed, put through the mangle, wrung,

5.4
'Hung out to dry; done like a kipper.'
'Oh, right then, you'll have had your chips …'
'I haven't been inside a chipper
For ages. I won't let those lips
Be high-cholesterol consumers.
I now eat pasta; and satsumas.
And don't do beef. I made the pledge
To give up meat and keep the veg.'
'Is this a Freudian confession?'
'Sod off! It's what I said it was.
I made a lifestyle choice because
I want my health. In my profession,
There's stress enough without the strain
Of failing health upon the brain.

5.5

'I fear arterial obstruction
That comes with saturated fat.
The rest's a matter of deduction.'
'In that case, I take off my hat
To you.' 'According to statistics,
Scots' most distinct characteristics
Are whisky, kilts and heart disease.'
'Is that the case? Two good from three's
Not bad. So, who's Luisa, Peter?'
'Someone at work.' 'At work?' 'Aye.' 'Right.
Is she the one who caused the fight?'
'No.' 'Oh, so are we going to meet her?'
'I'm not discussing this out here.
You fancy going for a beer?'

5.6

'Yes, but I think we should just sit here
And wait for Kim. She won't be long.'
'You're right. Exactly our remit here:
To sit quite still and do no wrong.'
Pete, leaning forward, starts untying
His bootlaces, but after trying,
In vain, to clear a double knot,
Gives up and sits back. 'Hell, it's not
Exactly the most sheltered spot here.
I'd totally forgotten how
Cold it gets. I remember now.
I've shivered since the day I got here.'
'And probably Kim's frosty glare
Has added to the icy air?'

5.7

'That too. I guess Kim's had a letter.
Shona and me … we've split up, Jim.
Christ, women do these things much better.
That's why I'm getting grief from Kim.
To take sides with one warring faction
Is just a simple gut reaction.
Her friend is hurt, she's lashing out
At who has caused it: me, no doubt.
I haven't come to seek alliance
With one or other. I would hate
To lay our fight upon your plate.
I thought the liberal appliance
Of alcohol, with friends back here,
Might make the sadness disappear.

5.8

'I know it's just a temporary
Measure, and it won't last the day,
But I'll do what is necessary
To make this feeling go away.
Let's change the subject. I won't bore you;
Place gory details out before you.'
With that, he gets up from his seat.
'So, Hearts v, Saints; win, draw, defeat?'
'Defeat. Through here, they always beat us.'
Jim answers him as if by rote.
'I wish I had my winter coat.
Hang on. There's something that might heat us.
I'll need to nip away for cash.
Back in a minute. Got to dash.'

5.9
Soon after, he's back with a pair of
Ridiculous Hey-Jimmy hats:
Two tartan tammies with the hair of
Two long-dead, long-haired ginger cats
Attached beneath. 'A tartan bonnet?
Just what we need. What's written on it?'
"C.U. Jimmy", "Scotland the Brave".'
'They were a bargain. The guy gave
Me two of them for eight pounds fifty;
And threw in a wee plastic flag,
A lion rampant, with the bag
For free. Is that not pretty nifty?'
'I think he saw you coming, Pete.'
'Who me? No, I'm much too discreet.'

5.10
He puts his hat on and is seated,
Then sees to it Jim follows suit.
'That's better. Now our heads are heated.'
But Jim's embarrassment's acute.
'Hey, Pete, I don't think I can bear this.
Someone I know might see me wear this.'
Pete laughs, and shouts at passers-by
'See you, Jimmy!' Jim gives a sigh
Bordering on exasperation.
'Is this how we are viewed abroad?'
Pete turns and gives a manic nod.
'No, seriously, as a nation,
Our impact, on the Richter scale
Of world affairs, would likely fail

5.11

'To register.' 'Your scale's defective.'
'It's not. I'll tell a tale which may
Help put it all into perspective.
St Andrew, Christ's apostle, lay
At rest, his ministry completed,
In ancient Greece. The Greeks defeated,
The heathen hordes were at the gate.
Afraid that they would desecrate
The grave, his relics were transported
To safe a place as could be found
—This was before the earth was round—
And thus St Andrew was escorted
Unto the farthest point of life,
The edges of the known world: Fife.

5.12

'No, really, that's as legend has it.
It's how St Andrews got its name.'
Jim, smiling at the story, as it
Appears to hold such small a grain
Of fact, it surely must be fiction,
Tries geographic contradiction.
'They couldn't find the Western Isles?
They're further by 200 miles.'
'They maybe got there on a Sunday,
St Andrew an unwelcome guest,
The Sabbath being the day of rest;
And, told to come back on the Monday,
Thought "Bugger this for a bad dream.
Let's take the boat to Pittenweem".

5.13
'Who knows? Although in total fairness,
Among the folk I know who take
An interest in such things, awareness
Of Scotland's gradual outbreak
Of devolutionary fervour
Is high. To the informed observer,
A parallel is clearly seen
Between the Catalonian scene
And ours. Think: self-determination,
But limited in scope and rule
From southern capital; old school
Establishment at every station;
Allegiance sworn to Church and King;
All more conservative, right-wing.

5.14
'Blaming Madrid for all their ailments;
By Madrilenes, thought to be
Mean-spirited, seasoned complainants.
Ring any bells? It does with me.'
'Informed observers? Are there many?
I didn't think there would be any
Within the circles you frequent.
It's very rare that you're content
To spend your rest and recreation
In lengthy and informed debate
On subjects like the nation's state.
Past limits of deliberation
For you were women, football, booze.
You've changed. Since when did you have views?'

5.15

'Since always. They've not found expression
Up until now, that's all. A few
Of us from work have a wee session
Now and again. And, yes we do
Talk about football, though the ladies
Would send us to the fires of Hades
If who was going to win the cup
Remained the only subject up
For conversation. 'Are they Spanish,
Your drinking buddies, or all Brits?'
'A mix of both: whoever fits
Into the group. It can be clannish
At times; the locals tend to stick
Together, with the ex-pats thick

5.16

As thieves. Though English, by tradition,
Is used at work. We all make do.'
'So who's brought out the politician
In you, then?' 'Oh, that would be Lou.'
'Who's he?' 'She's from Andalucia.
Came up north with her mate, Maria,
For the Olympics '92,
And stayed on.' 'Does she work with you?'
'IT. Systems support technician.
A subcontractor, but she's been
Permanent on the social scene
Since I've been there. It's her tuition
That's meant I'm caught less unawares
When small-talk turns to world affairs.

5.17
'Or even just to local matters
In Barcelona or Madrid.
My self-respect's not left in tatters
By some ambitious, smart-arsed kid
Bombarding me with bluff and blethers,
Preening pretentious peacock feathers
In some self-satisfied display
Of pre-pubescent cabaret.'
'That's youth for you: all drive, ambition;
A hormone-fuelled juggernaut
Oblivious to measured thought.
I guess you think your own position
Is under threat from youthful verve?
I think I might have touched a nerve!'

5.18
He laughs. 'Well, Sherlock, your detective
Methods have my Achilles heel.
My best defences are defective
If you can tell the way I feel.
But that's oversimplification
Of what's a complex situation.
I'm giving far too much away,
And now I don't know what to say.
My faculties are surely failing.
I wish I had your common sense
And wasn't quite so bloody dense.'
He stands and crosses to the railing,
And gazes downwards, and around
The Gardens, over to the Mound.

5.19
'You're just a little disaffected
With life just now. You've sense enough.
You always have been well respected,
Without all this awareness stuff.'
'Who, me?' 'Yes, you.' 'Huh, now you tell me.
This revelation may impel me
To question your sobriety.'
'Pete, there is no dubiety
About it.' 'But my life is rootless
Now that Shona and Josh have gone,
I've nothing left to build it on.
Each day has turned into a fruitless
Search for meaning; to find a role
To soothe my sad, uncertain soul.'

5.20
'To find a role? God, you were twenty
The last time I heard that from you.
If I remember, there were plenty
Willing to help you find one, too,
You thought the female population
Would be the route to your salvation.
Whether, of course, they thought the same
Is source of claim and counter-claim.
Egged on by unrestrained libation,
Your carnal passions did bestride
The Students' Union at Strathclyde
Each Friday, wreaking devastation
Upon the unsuspecting fleet
Of Glasgow's virginal elite.

5.21

'I envied you that bright and breezy
Manner, that cool and unforced charm
That seemed to render it so easy
To put a girl on to your arm.
We'd stand around like party-poopers,
Drinking ourselves into such stupors,
Attempting to blank out the pain
Of going home alone again.'
'I thought you lot just liked your bevvy?'
'Well, that was absolutely true.
We had a rare old night or two.
But it all got a wee bit heavy.
We soon grew out of it. Moved on
To other things. Kim came along

5.22

And changed the way my life was headed.'
'It's strange how these things turn out, Jim.
For all the girls I might have bedded,
I envied what you had with Kim.
You had a substance sadly lacking
In my affairs. Beyond the sacking,
I really didn't have much clue
What I should feel, or say, or do.'
'In truth, Pete, if you only knew it,
None of us did … or very few.
The bulk of us just muddled through,
And it was always you who blew it.'
'I guess; well, that was just the way
I was back then. Still am today

5.23
'By all accounts. Perhaps we're fated
To re-enact mistakes ad in-
Finitum; free will subjugated
By some obscure encephalin;
Lives pre-ordained by flaws genetic;
Attempts to change, therefore, pathetic,
And doomed to failure. I, perchance,
Am victim of mere circumstance.'
'A victim? You? You're just a chancer.
You can't, with credibility,
Deny responsibility.
To be resigned to fate's no answer.
You must believe that you can change
The world you're in, to rearrange

5.24
'Those things which cause you such vexation.
Make out a list; prioritise
Them in degrees of irritation.
Then verbalise and analyse.
It might give you some inspiration
To help explain your motivation.'
'I've been on that course.' 'What? Oh right.
I'm sorry, that was really trite.'
'Ten steps to business heaven? Jesus,
Does corporate man never sleep?
That junk's enough to make you weep.
These overvalued pedants tease us
With brainless bullshit, tripe and trash,
Then piss off, pockets full of cash.

5.25

'And change the world? Now look who's talking.'
'Aye. Years ago, we thought we could.'
'Excuse me, big man, but you're blocking
The road. Move over if you would
Be kind enough, and see that bunnet?
I wouldnae wear that if I'd won it!'
Pete turns around. 'My bunnet's bad?
Yours makes you look like your old dad.'
'How goes it, mate!' 'Jim!' 'Dod McPherson!'
'Who let him through passport control?'
'Not me.' 'You just out on parole?'
'Hey, I'm a professional person,
I'll have you know.' 'You're on the game?
Times must be hard. Myself, I blame

5.26

The parents.' 'Right.' 'How long you here for?'
'A flying visit; nearly done.'
'You didn't fancy going to cheer for
Your team? Not your idea of fun?'
'That started off as the intention,
Till his wife made an intervention.'
'Well, you were lucky. It was shite.
I've got some pizza. Want a bite?
Cheese, pepperoni, extra chillies.'
'How did it finish?' 'I don't know;
I left with half an hour to go.
We scored a cracker; Ricky Gillies
Free kick; other than that, a bore.
I left when Hearts scored number four.'

5.27

'This bunnet's going in the midden.'
'Behave. You need your Buddies' hat.
Besides, it keeps your bald bit hidden.'
'Thanks for reminding me of that.'
'Here, swap.' Pete takes the bunnet from him
And puts the Tam o' Shanter on him.
'Transplants? No problem; head of hair
By Pete & Jimmy leisurewear!'
'Thanks, guys, just what I wanted.' 'Still with
The same firm?' 'No, moved on, must be
Two years ago. I couldn't see
A future; started to take ill with
The culture of uncertainty
And rumours of redundancy;

5.28

'Cost-cutting measures; all purporting
To be a part of something new.
I took a package; it's supporting
Me through a college course; I've two
Months left until my graduation:
Landscape design and renovation.
Less money, like, but we'll get by.
What time is it? I'll need to fly.
I said I'd meet Pat at the station.
You headed home?' 'We're stuck here.' 'Why?'
'Waiting for Kim', the joint reply.
'Kim? Pass on my felicitations.
Listen, we could meet up tonight?
We plan to go out for a bite:

5.29

The Watermill. If you can make it,
Magic; if not, best wishes, Pete.
Love Street next week, Jim. Can you take it?'
'Yeah, go on, then. You want to meet?'
'I'll phone.' 'Och, we'll come in past later.'
'I'll keep you seats. My boy's a waiter.'
With that, he turns and heads towards
Waverley, lost among the hordes
Of travellers, last-minute shoppers,
Of tourists trying to find their way
To B&Bs, pre-booked, to stay;
Of coteries of captious coppers,
Whose task, to send supporters back
To Paisley, on well-beaten track,

5.30

Will likely be discharged by teatime,
As there are few supporters through,
Resulting in extended free time
To do the things policemen do.
          Whatever that is ... This is getting
          A bit off subject. Oh, stop fretting.
          I need a break. My pen's run out;
          My head is sore. I've got a bout
          Of influenza, or a virus.
          I need a fortnight in the sun.
          How long has this tale still to run?
          I'm running out of lined papyrus;
          I'm needing specs, I've gone cross-eyed.
          I work all day. My brain is fried.

5.31
When I get home, my poor wee body
Is needing rest, and more beside.
I know: I'll pour myself a toddy,
A dram to make me warm inside.
That lot in Princes Street can stay there.
I no longer control the way their
Weekend is going anyway;
My plans for it had gone agley
Six hours ago. And me the author ...
I've lost the plot. I'm walnut-whipped.
They've gone and written their own script,
The buggers; after all that bother;
But then, I've been with them this far,
I'd best go back ... see how they are.

5.32
No sign of Kim. They sit. 'You've got to
Admire him for his courage, but;
It must be fifteen years he's fought to
Build a career; and now, he's cut
All ties to a secure existence,
And ditched the means of his subsistence.'
'Perhaps, but I've been skint before.
No fun, the wolf outside your door.'
'But don't you ever get frustrated?'
'Oh, roughly, every single day.
I wish I could just walk away
From all the superannuated
Responsibilities that keep
Us turning up each day, like sheep.

5.33
But, then again, it's advantageous
To have the wherewithal to pay
The bills. Insolvency's contagious.'
'I know. It's funny, though. The way
Ambitions couldn't be much bolder
When we set out. Then, we get older.
We grow conservative, afraid
Of losing everything we've made.
We hide away rogue aspirations.
Faint-hearted, mortgaged to the hilt,
We cling to what's already built;
And thus, denied articulation,
The dreams on which our hearts were set
Wither, and turn in to regret.'

5.34
'Hey, Jim?' 'What?' 'Why are you so cheerful?'
'My happy nature, I expect.
I'll take the hint; you've had an earful.'
'I wish I'd been an architect.'
'That's news to me. Again.' 'To find you
Had something real to leave behind you;
Some record of your time on earth …
What must a job like that be worth?
But me, if I dropped dead tomorrow,
What would I leave behind to show
That I existed? Who would know?
The final measure, to my sorrow,
The life and work of this poor man:
One fully paid-up pension plan.'

5.35
'Paid up to date? Well, that's a bonus.
It wouldn't do, for any sake,
To pop your clogs and leave the onus
On others to finance your wake.'
'Hmm, that was just a touch sardonic,
I find the whole thing so ironic.
I'm worth more six feet under than
Sat here with you. What price this man?'
'Okay, how many folk, however,
Do leave an imprint? Precious few,
I'd warrant. And of those who do,
So what? They still don't live for ever.
Our lot on earth is transient.
No high-fallutin' monument

5.36
Will alter that.' 'But I'm not trying
To overcome mortality,
To live for ever. Not denying
The simple, bleak finality
Of what's in store, but when I get there,
I'm terrified of being met there
By inconsolable regret,
Discovering the epithet
That most applies to my achievements,
My Herculean efforts to
Contribute to this life, is 'Who?'
And who would suffer the bereavement?
Would any weep with heavy heart?'
'I'll give you two names for a start.'

5.37
'I doubt it, Jim. My reputation
With Josh and Shona's pretty low.'
'Slight problem with communication:
I meant us two, but there you go.
Shona and Josh I took for granted.
I doubt your favour's been supplanted
Whatever's happened; and, what's more,
That takes the number up to four!
Then this Luisa is another;
There's Dod and Pat; all our old mates,
The lager-swilling reprobates;
And don't forget your dear old mother.
Alive, you gave her grief for years,
So, dead, you can't deny her tears.

5.38
'How many's that? It must be twenty.
That's not including all the guys
You know from work. That will be plenty
To celebrate your sad demise!'
'It really is such consolation
To know that my annihilation
Would give so many the excuse
To party; that it should induce
Such celebration.' 'Oh, stop whingeing.'
'I need a sympathetic ear,
In absence of a bloody beer;
Though shopping seems to be impinging
On all my plans in that respect;
No sign of Kim yet, I expect?'

5.39
'No sign. We could erect a statue
In honour of your mortal fate.'
'I get the slightest feeling that you
Don't take this seriously, mate.'
'Oh really? What gives that impression?'
'I'm sinking into deep depression.
I'm perched atop a vast abyss,
And you just sit and take the piss.
Some mate you are.' 'As I was saying,
'We'll build it by Scott's monument,
Or down beside the Parliament;
Or Calton Hill. You'd stand, surveying
The vista from the Parthenon
For ever more.' 'What drug you're on

5.40
I don't know, but I sure don't want you
To leave me up there on my own.
Do that and I'll come back and haunt you.'
'I gather, Peter, from your tone,
You find the notion diabolic?'
'I sure do. While perhaps symbolic
Of ancient, democratic roots
And philosophical pursuits,
It's all a front; an ostentatious
Fake fur, lording it over Leith,
And with no knickers underneath.
No thanks. But if you'd be so gracious
As to erect me, if you would,
Within the brand new Holyrood.

5.41
I'd find the comfort there sufficient!'
'I bet you would. The management
Of public money's inefficient.
That budget's millions overspent.
A giant site was excavated
And crates of cash, appropriated
From simple, law-abiding souls
Like me, were poured into the holes.'
'I know. The same the whole world over.
Your penny-wise accountant's soul
May find the lack of cost control
Intolerable. But from Dover
To John o' Groats to Timbuktu,
Our taxes disappear from view

5.42
'At speeds that make a hot-arsed cheetah
Seem sluggish as a snail in shit.'
'While some live out La Dolce Vita
Entirely on the back of it,
No doubt.' 'Most likely, but don't judge it
On that alone. I don't begrudge it
In many ways. Some said the same
When Barca put in for the Games
In '92. They thought it funny;
A chance to sit and patronise.
Had they the skills to organise?
Where would they find such sums of money?
They'd break the bank; they'd lose their nerve.
Instead, with confidence and verve,

5.43
It turned into an affirmation
Of Catalan identity;
An optimistic celebration
Held high for all the world to see.
The city was rejuvenated,
New opportunities created.
Need I say more? You listening, Jim?'
He doesn't hear. He's spotted Kim.
'I wasn't sure you'd still be waiting.'
'As if we wouldn't. We've been sat
Watching the world, chewing the fat.'
'What subjects have you been debating?'
'Oh, all the big stuff: life and death …'
Kim, heavy laden, out of breath,

5.44
Sits down, depositing her parcels
Beside her, kicking off her shoes.
'Oh, my poor, aching metatarsals.'
'I have a cure for that: it's booze.'
'Oh, really?' 'Yes, I'm sure I read it
Somewhere. Some paediatrician said it.'
'A paediatrician?' 'Yes, you know,
A doctor for the foot and toe.'
She turns in mock exasperation
To Pete, who covers up his eyes
And shakes his head. 'He mortifies
Me sometimes.' 'Just degeneration
Of brain cells, Kim. It's commonplace
In older men.' 'Oh, shut your face.

5.45

'Let's go. I need some lubrication.'
'Let's just get home. Forget the beer.
I need help with the decoration.
Kate's room. Tomorrow, she'll be here.'
'Since when?' 'She phoned me just this morning.'
'You never said!' 'What, you need warning?'
'For Christ's sake. Well, I've news for you.
John phoned me and he's coming too.'
'You didn't say!' 'You weren't talking
To me this afternoon!' 'Oh, right.
So it's my fault we have to fight?
'Guys,' Pete stands up, and slowly walking
Away, says 'Just off round the block.
I think, perhaps, you two should talk.'

Chapter 6

The evening's curious commotions

6.1
Wallpapering: a long, painstaking
And purgatorial pursuit,
Invented as a way of making
A man's contrition absolute.
The sin, routinely unspecific,
Redeemed by penance soporific.
Thus, Jim surveys the waiting wall,
And gulps two paracetamol.
His head is sore, his eyes are popping,
Afflictions not entirely new
To wage-slaves of the VDU.
Perhaps it was the pain of shopping.
He's thought for ages to invest
Some cash in an ophthalmic test,

6.2
But has not yet achieved this mission,
Preferring to believe such ills
Will clear without need of optician
Being called to demonstrate his skills.
He's sure his healthy constitution
Provides the best long-term solution.
And, given time, will soon restore
Him to full fitness, as before.
A typically male reaction,
In Kim's view: just ignore the thing
That causes all the worrying,
And hope that diligent inaction
Will make it simply disappear.
But, then again, perhaps it's fear,

6.3
As, imperceptibly, time passes,
Until the day we realise
The reason that we're needing glasses:
The ageing process on the eyes.
The implications soon confound us;
The institutions which surround us,
Which give a reassuring sense
Of fundamental permanence
And meaning to our vegetating,
Short-sighted intellects, are seen
Quite suddenly, to just have been
No more than self-perpetuating,
And powerless to help delay
Our individual decay;

6.4
Acknowledgement thus signifying
Acceptance; ageing with good grace.
The option, simply put: denying
The whole event is taking place,
Though in the long term counteractive,
Seems at the moment more attractive.
Kim cuts a dozen lengths to size.
Jim starts to paste, and really tries
His best to be enthusiastic.
He makes a joke. 'Saturday night
Wallpapering. What a delight.'
But Kim thinks he's just being sarcastic,
And snatches at the roll he's done.
'Well, it's not my idea of fun

6.5

'Either, you know. We have to do this
Tonight. We can't allow our Kate
To come back home and have to view this
Pigsty. Anyway, at this rate,
It won't take long. Here, paste these pieces.'
With that, the conversation ceases,
And they, amidst well-practised hush,
Work on in tandem. Jim, with brush,
Applies adhesive per directive,
And wonders what's become of Pete,
Deposited back down the street
Some time ago, with clear objective:
One chicken curry, with boiled rice,
Sweet and sour king prawns, with chips … twice.

6.6

As time goes by, Jim's belly rumbles,
Deprived of food for hours on end.
'So where's he got to, then?' he grumbles.
'Well, I don't know. He is your friend.'
'Yours too.' 'I know. What was he saying
This afternoon? Was he portraying
Poor Shona as the one to blame?'
'No, not at all. In fact, his name
Is mud, according to his version
Of things. But, really, I can't tell.
He hides his feelings far too well.'
'I'll try some feminine coercion
When he gets back.' 'Oh, God,
Be gentle with the hapless sod.'

6.7

'I will. My middle name is "Gentle".'
Jim looks, with disbelieving eye.
'It's Okay, I won't be judgemental,
But I must know the reasons why.'
'We've been around this block too often.
I think age has begun to soften
Our attitudes to wrong and right.
These things are rarely black and white;
In any case, blame's incidental.
What's gained by allocating fault,
Or launching self-righteous assault,
That's likely to be detrimental
To all concerned? That much, we know
Quite well enough. Though why we show

6.8

'Such calm, mature consideration
To others, yet where we're concerned,
Are quick to offer condemnation,
Beats me. You'd think we might have learned
Some way of reaching a consensus;
Developed skills in mending fences;
Instead of building barricades
And lobbing verbal hand grenades
At one another, slowly wreaking
Havoc on our relationship,
In pointless acts of brinkmanship;
Or worse the days of hardly speaking;
It wasn't always quite the way
It seems to be for us, today.

6.9
'Too often, things are left unspoken.'
'What's prompted you to now express
Your feelings? Is it just a token
Gesture, this burst of openness?'
'Kim, my semantics may be artless,
But don't think I've become a heartless,
Cold-blooded, calculating man.
My heart's as hard as marzipan.
I wish our warring ways were ended,
That's all. The day I've had today,
Plus all that Pete has had to say,
I think it's high time we attended
What matters most to us, before
It disappears for evermore.'

6.10
It's quite beyond his understanding
How far he's travelled on the route
He'd set out on, at length, crash-landing,
Without the aid of parachute,
On unfamiliar territory
Not shown on his itinerary.
The signs are Greek, and hard to see;
Call out the AA, RAC.
They'll come if his account's in credit.
How is his heart's financial state?
Let's see … is he paid up to date?
Now, where did he direct that debit?
His standing order's fallen flat.
So no insurance. Well, that's that;

6.11
His pigeon loft is bare and waiting,
But homing instinct he has none.
And so, he sits there vacillating,
And worries that his doo is done.
When we lose all sense of direction,
Where should we look for resurrection?
Just take a leap of faith and fly?
We might end up as pigeon pie.
Resorting to ornithomancy
In time of stress, though, is absurd,
As, after all, he's not a bird,
In spite of all his flights of fancy.
Apart from one fact, overlooked:
His goose may well be truly cooked.

6.12
'In the beginning, what attracted
Us to each other, Kim?' 'For me,
The way you looked, and smiled, and acted;
So full of life and energy;
But now, the smile appears truncated;
The energy is dissipated.'
'I look the same.' 'That's what you think.
You do, but only when I drink!'
'Ha! Ha! My energy's expended
On work, and keeping us alive.
I get up every day and strive.'
'I know, I know, don't be offended,
I'm only joking. I'm the same.
In that respect, you're free of blame.

6.13
'But not one other, which is taking
For granted that I'm always here.'
'Who, me?' 'You asked; I'm simply making
My feelings on the matter clear.
For nigh on twenty years together,
I've felt my status slowly wither,
From equal, true love, special friend,
To unpaid servant, left to tend
The needs of others, subjugating
My thoughts and feelings to their good.
How lovely if, just once, I could
See some of you reciprocating
The care I've shown, to make it plain
That all these years were not in vain.

6.14
The kids no longer needing mothered,
I've lost all sense of who I am.
My whole identity's been smothered.
I can't tell if you give a damn.'
'I do, but can they be recaptured:
Those heady days when young, enraptured,
We lived a life of vacant bliss
And measured time from kiss to kiss?'
'No, but it's grown so melancholic;
It shouldn't have to be this bad.
What were the feelings you once had?
Was your attraction just hydraulic?'
'I, simply, just quite fancied you.
And, to be honest, I still do.

6.15

'Kim, it was never my intention
To treat you with such disregard,
Or offer you such scant attention,
But, sometimes, it's so very hard
To find release from worldly pressure,
That seeps across the bounds of leisure
And through my dreams at dead of night,
Till early dawn, without respite.
I've tried to deal with it by blocking
The outside world from getting through,
But found those closest blocked out too.
And I don't know if simply talking
Can mend the damage that's been done.'
'I don't know; but you have made one

6.16

'Small movement in the right direction,
By letting your defences fall.
To know the cause of your dejection,
To realise it wasn't all
My fault, is such a revelation.
You never gave me indication.
I feared you found me ugly, fat,
Unlovable.' 'No, never that.
I think I, too, have lost all notion
Of who I am, and want to be.
The stuffing's been knocked out of me.
My motivation, my devotion,
For years was based round Kate and John.
But, now they've both grown up and gone,

6.17
'I've lost my purpose as a father;
And husband, too, from what you said.'
'Don't get yourself in such a lather.
How could such nonsense fill your head?
I miss the fact that I don't see their
Faces each day. Our job's to be there
If needed, as I'm sure you are:
You've still to buy them both a car!'
'Oh, God, I'm chained to work; cemented.
The lemming-like brutality
Of corporate mentality
Will have me, very soon, demented.
I'll need to have a word with Dod;
He's got it sussed, the jammy sod.

6.18
'He's packed it in, jumped ship, defected;
Though how he's going to make ends meet …'
'That might be sooner than expected.
Is that him coming up the street?'
'It is an' all. We're for a visit.
Pete's brought a houseful.' 'What time is it?
They can't come in. Look at the mess.
I'll need to disappear, get dressed
In something smarter, for a party.
A different top, clean underwear;
Then put my face on, do my hair.
I can't have people see me clarty.
Here, finish this.' 'What, me?' 'Yes, you.
There're only two bits left to do.'

6.19
She rushes off. Jim flings the pieces
Of pasted paper on the wall,
Then evens out the bumps and creases.
'There's nothing to this lark at all.'
Out on the doorstep, someone's singing.
It's followed by the doorbell ringing.
He runs downstairs and lets them in.
'Dod. Pat! How are you? Bill and Lynne!
'Is this okay, Jim?' 'Sure, don't worry.'
'We met Pete earlier tonight;
Assured us it would be all right.'
'Ah, Pete.' 'Jim, I forgot the curry.
These people dragged me to the pub.
You're not still waiting for your grub?"

6.20
'We dragged you?' 'Slight exaggeration
On my part. Well, the afternoon
I suffered gave me dehydration.
I couldn't get a drink too soon.
I don't suppose this mortal sinner
Has any chance of getting dinner?'
'If you had learned to navigate
Your way beyond a pub door, mate,
You'd not be stood here looking famished.'
'Guilty as charged. I'll need to try
To feed myself some humble pie.'
'Shut up!' 'Kim!' 'Pete, we thought you'd vanished.
Hello, this is a nice surprise;
Pat, Dod; Lynne … didn't recognise

6.21
'You there at all. You look completely
Different. You've changed your hair; lost weight.'
I could have put that more discretely,
Thinks Kim. Oh, well. 'You're looking great!'
'Thanks. My instructor keeps my posture
Ship-shape. At our age, to have lost your
Figure and looks is just neglect.
It shows a lack of self-respect.'
Pat turns to Kim. 'I've kept my figure.
I think I'm looking pretty trim
These days. Do you not think so, Kim?'
'I do.' 'I won't get any bigger,
Because we can't afford to eat.
He'll have us all out on the street

6.22
In no time.' 'Christ, I don't believe it;
Can you not give me bloody peace?
Just for this evening? Can't you leave it
Alone? Just for tonight at least?'
Pat bursts into a tearful torrent.
'My fears are real, and they don't warrant
Me being spoken to like that.'
She runs into the kitchen. 'Pat—'
Kim follows her. Dod doesn't risk it.
Nor do the others, save for Pete,
Who, mindful of the need to eat,
Goes through and asks Kim for a biscuit,
Returning pleased as punch with three
Buttered digestives for his tea.

6.23
An awkward silence is averted
By Dod, who passes round some beer.
'I'm sorry, guys. Should have alerted
You to the difficulties here.
That quite unseemly demonstration
Of temper is the cumulation
Of two years' conflict, ever since
I started trying to convince
Pat that my life was unfulfilling;
The nine to five had made me stale.
My pleading was to no avail.
I only wish she'd be more willing
To even try to share my dream.'
'She's scared of being skint, you mean.

6.24
'If you did that to me, I'd leave you.'
'Don't tempt me, Lynne.' 'I mean it, Bill.
I wouldn't stand for it. I'd heave you
Out of the marriage bed until
Your hell-bent ways had been repented,
And normal service implemented.
Don't get ideas in your head;
Your motivation's comfort-led.'
'That's me told, then. I've no intention
Of packing in the day job, though.
I'm happy with the job I know.'
'What's that, Bill?' 'Oh, didn't he mention?
He hides his light under a bush;
Senior partner; Toilette and Douche.'

6.25
'For Pete's sake, Lynne.' 'I'm not complaining …'
'I don't mean you. Time we were home.'
'Don't go! It's all so entertaining!'
'Oh, shut up, Pete, you little gnome!'
Lynne storms out. 'Pete, a small suggestion.
Is some decorum out the question?'
'Not his fault, Jim, Lynne's out of line.
She's had a little too much wine;
An incidence that's been increasing
In frequency of late, I fear.'
'Don't worry, you're among friends here.'
'I've had it up to here, policing
The drunken, rambling blatherskite;
The first one hundred times, I might

6.26
'Have found it funny, or capricious;
But it's not funny anymore.
It makes her incoherent, vicious,
A fractious and ill-mannered bore.'
Pete sits there, fingers drumming, restive,
And finishes his last digestive.
'Toilette and Douche? They're based in Cannes?
I heard they had gone down the pan!'
'Bog standard case of obsolescence,'
Adds Dod. Jim casts a nervous glance
At Bill. 'Huh. Sympathy? Fat chance
From these retarded adolescents.'
On which sarcastic note, the four
Dissolve in laughter on the floor.

6.27
Through in the kitchen, Pat's been pouring
Her heartfelt worries out to Kim.
'He's spent the last two years ignoring
Everything that I've said to him.
My every argument rejected,
Our future now lies unprotected.
We'd just begun to feel secure.
That he should make me now endure
This speculative expedition …'
Lynne bursts in. 'Pat, love, there's no doubt,
You should just throw the bastard out,
If he puts you in this position.'
'It's not as plain as that, alas.'
Kim goes and gets another glass,

6.28
And settles down to hear Pat's saga.
Lynne soon gets bored, and drains her glass.
'I love your kitchen. We've an Aga.
It brings a little touch of class.'
Kim looks at her, and nods, politely.
Pat's not disposed to treat fools lightly
Tonight. 'Why don't you light the gas
And shove your Aga up your arse?'
'Lads, can you see from where I'm coming?
You understand it, I can tell.
You must have had the urge as well?
She's worried that we'll end up slumming.
We won't, but so what if we do?
There's more to life than money. True?'

6.29

In tentative and unconvincing
Agreement, each one nods assent.
Dod frets a little at evincing
Such mild support for his intent.
'She might come round yet.' 'Definately.'
'She's not shown signs of coming lately.'
Pete looks at Jim. Bill feigns a cough,
But starts to laugh. 'Oh, bugger off!'
'So: partner, Bill? You must be loaded.'
'Suppose I am: enough to feed
Ourselves and pay for what we need.'
'How much d'you make?' 'Bill, don't be goaded
Into revealing the amount.'
'Probably struggles to keep count.'

6.30

'I do. To keep track of her spending.
Of late, the credit card's red hot.
It seems the spree is never-ending.
I couldn't even tell you what
She spends it on. It takes her mind off
Things.' 'Is she working?' 'Well, she's signed off.
It's been three months. Stuff going on
I don't want to expand upon.'
'No worries.' 'I've been fraternising
With a good friend of yours.' 'Oh aye?
Who's that, then?' 'Your boss, John McKay.
Speaks well of you.' 'That patronising …'
'Seemed to appear out of thin air,
But now he pops up everywhere.

6.31
'He's joined the golf club, church, Round Table.'
'Hey, Bill, do they just meet at Knights?'
'Who?' 'Just ignore him. He's unstable.'
'It's lack of food. My appetite's
Not satisfied by three wee buttered
Digestive biscuits.' 'You're half-guttered.'
'I know. Why don't you just phone down,
And have them bring some curries round?'
'I think I might. I haven't eaten
Myself. I'll ask the girls if they
Want, too.' He stands and makes his way
Towards the kitchen, but is beaten
To it. Pat crashes through the door
And drags Lynne down on to the floor.

6.32
Kim quickly has them separated,
Helped straight away by Dod and Bill.
They're soon, in different rooms, placated,
Though Lynne complains of feeling ill.
'Come on. Let's go before you throw up.
I'm sorry Kim, we had to show up
And cause such trouble.' 'It's okay.
I know, sometimes, things get this way.
I'll phone a taxi.' 'No, she's needing
Fresh air. We'll get one up the street.
Jim, phone me sometime, and we'll meet.'
Lynne turns around. Her lip is bleeding.
'Yes, come and visit sometime.' 'When?'
'We'll phone.' 'Right; see you sometime, then.'

6.33
Declining offers of a dressing,
They make their exit. Meanwhile, Pat
Sits on the bedroom floor, caressing
A bruise upon her arm. The cat,
Who's missed out on the altercation,
Comes strolling through, in indignation
That no one's paid her any heed,
Announcing that she wants a feed.
'The service here is really shoddy,'
Says Pete to cat. 'Take my advice:
Go elsewhere for your fish fried rice.'
Pat says to Kim, 'Please can somebody
Arrange a cab? We can't impose.
What you must think of us, God knows.'

6.34
Ten minutes later, they've departed.
'Great party, you guys! Take a bow!
'Right, Pete. I haven't even started
On you yet, but I aim to now.'
Kim grabs his collar and propels him
Into the kitchen, where she tells him:
'I heard from Shona, just today.
Now tell me what you have to say.
The truth, and all things appertaining.
My friend is devastated. Why?'
He flinches visibly. 'Well, I
Have trouble, sometimes, in explaining …'
'Come off it, Pete. You're just a louse.'
Jim goes and phones the Hong Kong House.

6.35
He's found his appetite diminish,
By this late hour. Two, between three,
Will do. He goes upstairs to finish
Clearing Kate's room of the debris.
It's quickly back in prime condition,
And he begins to reposition
The chest of drawers, bed, wardrobe, chair,
Plus one redundant teddy bear,
Where they had been. The restoration
Complete, he takes a moment to
Admire the end result. The view
Turns pride to sudden trepidation:
A perfect pattern all around,
Save for two bits, hung upside down.

6.36
Perhaps it might escape detection?
Perhaps King Billy might be Pope;
A eunuch might have an erection;
And Einstein might have been a dope.
He thinks, with the onset of terror,
How to eradicate the error.
The wardrobe's moved across the floor,
But ends up too close to the door.
He can't envisage a solution.
And tells himself, in self-defence
'Not like it's a hanging offence.
But still, there may be retribution.
I'm done for, and I fear the worst;
I'll hope for my last supper first.

6.37
'Suppose I could just feign indifference,
Pretend it never caught my eye.'
The doorbell signals his deliverance.
He runs downstairs and pays the guy
His dues, with minimum of chatter.
Out from the kitchen comes a clatter
Of forks and knives and china plates.
Jim wanders through to join his mates.
Pete turns away at Jim's appearance.
Kim motions with her eyes to Jim,
But finds her meaning lost on him.
'So, you've survived her interference?
Come on, let's eat. The curry's here.
I'll serve. Kim, pass Pete out a beer.'

6.38
'Not hungry, Jim, I couldn't eat it.'
He turns around. His eyes are red.
'The cat can have it, or re-heat it
Tomorrow. I'm off up to bed.'
'Not hungry? Pete, I don't believe it!
You are the one who …' 'Jim, just leave it.'
'Jim, pal, we don't appreciate
What we have got, till it's too late.
Where will I sleep?' 'Kate's room. I'll show you.'
'I really envy you two guys.'
At that, to Jim's complete surprise,
Pete hugs him, roughly. 'Good to know you,
Old son.' He turns around to Kim
And says, 'Come on, then. Tuck me in.'

6.39
Jim dishes out the sweet and sours.
Kim comes back down. They start to eat,
And end up sitting there for hours,
Dissecting details of deceit,
Discussing friends and shared emotions,
The evening's curious commotions;
How some unmentionable clown
Had hung wallpaper upside down.
In bed, the duo rediscover
The hushed delights of silent sex
—Lest careless cadence resurrects
Their friend from underneath his cover—
Until, in tired and tangled heap,
The pair, at length, fall fast asleep.

Epilogue

Guys,
Sorry, I've a train needs catching.
This B&B is really crap:
The wallpaper's not even matching,
And breakfast … cold prawns in a bap?
I sneaked out early without paying.
Kim, yes, I hear what you are saying.
P.S The bedsprings put a hex
On your attempts at silent sex,
But glad to hear you're both still able!
My love to all,
Your old friend,
Pete.

Kim crosses to the window seat
And lays the note upon the table.
Then curls up, sleepily, to wait
For sight or sound of John and Kate.

Acknowledgements

CD *advised of flawed synopsis;*

GW, *where rightful nook*
For commas, colons and full-stops is;

HS *quite simply blitzed the book*
And warmed to Kim, though sought firm pledges
Re. smoothing some of Jim's rough edges.

X *left me in unpublished state,*
But said "Don't give up: this this tale's great!"

JY, *when doubt was coursing through me,*
Just penned a note which said "Jim, look:
It's good enough to be a book."

And last, not least, those closest to me,
Who choose to put up with — thank God —
This well-intentioned, simple sod.

Also from Boorach Books:

Illustrated books for children:

Granny Baggy   *Written by Jim Blyth,
illustrated by Tanja Russita*

Who is John?   *Written & illustrated by
Tanja Russita, English version by Jim Blyth.*

Books for grumpy Grandpas:

Govan to Garthdee*: Selected Poems of Ken
Fittman*

*Have a peek inside - all of the above books are
available to view at Amazon.co.uk*